THE HOUSE AT
HOMECOMING COVE

Ginny Baird

*To Thelma Banzhoff —
Congrats and happy
reading!
Ginny Baird*

THE HOUSE AT HOMECOMING COVE

Published by
Winter Wedding Press

Copyright © 2015
Ginny Baird
Trade Paperback
ISBN 978-1-942058-11-3

Edited by Martha Trachtenberg
Proofread by Sally Knapp
Cover by Dar Albert

About the Author

From the time she could talk, romance author Ginny Baird was making up stories, much to the delight—and consternation—of her family and friends. By grade school, she'd turned that inclination into a talent, whereby her teacher allowed her to write and produce plays rather than write boring book reports. Ginny continued writing throughout college, where she contributed articles to her literary campus weekly, then later pursued a career managing international projects with the U.S. State Department.

Ginny has held an assortment of jobs, including schoolteacher, freelance fashion model, and greeting card writer, and has published more than twenty works of fiction and optioned ten screenplays. She has also published short stories, nonfiction, and poetry, and admits to being a true romantic at heart.

Ginny is a *New York Times* and *USA Today* Bestselling Author of several books, including novellas in her Holiday Brides Series. She's a member of Romance Writers of America (RWA), the RWA Published Authors Network (PAN), and Novelists, Inc. (NINC).

When she's not writing, Ginny enjoys cooking, biking, and spending time with her family in Tidewater, Virginia. She loves hearing from her readers and welcomes visitors to her website at http://www.ginnybairdromance.com.

Books by Ginny Baird

Holiday Brides Series
The Christmas Catch
The Holiday Bride
Mistletoe in Maine
Beach Blanket Santa
Baby, Be Mine

Summer Grooms Series
Must-Have Husband
My Lucky Groom
The Wedding Wish
The Getaway Groom

Romantic Ghost Stories
The Ghost Next Door (A Love Story)
The Light at the End of the Road
The House at Homecoming Cove

Romantic Comedy
Real Romance
The Sometime Bride
Santa Fe Fortune
How to Marry a Matador
Counterfeit Cowboy
The Calendar Brides
My Best Friend's Bride

Bundles
Christmas Magic: The Complete Holiday Brides
Series (Books 1 – 5)
The Holiday Brides Collection (Books 1–4)
A Summer Grooms Selection (Books 1–3)
Real Romance and The Sometime Bride (Gemini
Edition)
Santa Fe Fortune and How to Marry a Matador
(Gemini Edition)
Wedding Bells Bundle

Short Stories
The Right Medicine (Short Story and Novel
Sampler)
Special Delivery (A Valentine's Short Story)

Ginny Baird's

THE HOUSE AT HOMECOMING COVE

The House at Homecoming Cove

Her words came out in a whisper. "Thank you for everything. For coming to my rescue, for..." She was saying goodbye, yet her chin tilted toward his and she took a step closer, her lips barely parted, inviting. She peered up at him and met his gaze with a look that was surprisingly heated, decidedly predatory. There was no mistaking it. Melissa wanted him too. That was all the encouragement Stone needed to take her in his arms and bring his mouth down on hers with a hungry desire that surpassed all expectations.

Melissa gasped with delight and sighed into his kiss. Stone's empty mug slid from her grasp and landed somewhere on the sofa. Stone pressed his eager body to hers and ran his hands up her back, threading his fingers through her hair. She was glorious, beautiful, her gaze sparking with reciprocal passion. Stone groaned and kissed her again, savoring the taste of her, delighting in the sweetness of her body molded to his, as his blood pumped harder and his heart beat like a kettledrum gone out of control. It was more than a kiss; it was like coming home.

"Stone," she said breathlessly. He opened his eyes to find his cheeks nestled between her palms.

She looked up at him her face flushed with longing. "I think you'd better go."

"Yeah," he said, his pulse pounding. "I'd better go."

Thunder boomed and rain slapped the windowpanes, while the fire hissed and moaned.

Neither one moved.

"Melissa," Stone whispered, brushing his lips over hers. "You and me... It's like... I don't know."

"I know," she replied, meeting his kiss. "I feel it too."

Chapter One

Melissa Carter opened the door to the century-old farmhouse and fell back a step at the onslaught of musty air. Autumn winds blew, rustling the gold and brown leaves on the tall oak overarching the building's stone stoop. Daylight was fading, causing the sky to take on a pinkish cast as dusk closed in. Melissa drew in a breath and pressed ahead, a large bag of groceries clutched in one arm. She'd been warned to bring supplies, as the nearest grocery store was more than thirty miles away, and she had. Boxes loaded with canned goods, rice, and pasta sat in the trunk of her SUV. She'd filled her cooler to the brim with meats and dairy products, and planned to freeze what she could for later. She'd also packed plenty of fresh fruits and vegetables to supplement her diet well into the next week. Then, she could think about venturing into the nearby town to purchase any incidental fill-in items. But basically, she was set. All she needed now was a piano.

Melissa stepped over the threshold and into the foyer of the sprawling old home. Heartpine floors shone beneath antique oriental rugs. The air smelled stale, but the floor was polished and things seemed in good order. Amazingly, nothing was caked with dust. The caretaker

Melissa had made arrangements with obviously did a good job of keeping up the place, even though it was scarcely occupied off season. Melissa peered into the dining room to her left, finding an old farm table big enough to accommodate twelve people positioned beside a wood-burning fireplace. She spied a kitchen center island straight ahead of her and a sink framed by a large window. But when Melissa turned to her right, she tightened her hold on the paper bag. The living room was breathtaking, with a huge comfy couch and side chairs, and two walls boasting enormous windows overlooking the water. The room was decorated with distressed furniture touches: an old sea trunk here, a weathered bookcase teeming with tomes there, and low end tables with impressive brass drawer pulls. Flickering light shimmered through beveled glass panes that appeared to be as old as the house, and she could see it bouncing off the sparkling cove, from which the property had taken its name. The House at Homecoming Cove sat on fifty acres of land on a portion of Virginia's Eastern Shore adjoining the Chesapeake Bay and its snarl of creeks and rivers. Small gusts of wind kicked up ripples across the glassy surface of the water, ringed on three sides by narrow, sandy banks and swaying trees.

Melissa walked toward the windows, mesmerized by the stunning natural beauty of her surroundings. She now saw this room also included a fireplace and had a back door that led to a wide screened porch overlooking a patio. A grassy stretch of land abutted a dock that extended into the water, and a private beach, accessible by a footpath from the patio, sat at the base of an embankment. The best part was that there wasn't another soul around. The house's caretaker, Captain

Bill, had assured her there was nowhere more remote in October than this part of Virginia. Melissa suddenly heard a sharp pinging sound like metal clanking against metal. She strode into the kitchen and set her bag down on the counter, trying to discern where the noise was coming from. The kitchen seemed modest but well appointed, its stainless steel appliances appearing nearly new. *Clank, clank, clank...* There it was again!

Melissa's eye caught on a structure outside the kitchen window. A barn was directly behind the house, so she'd failed to see it before. It sat maybe thirty feet from the main house beside a run-down garden surrounded by a white picket fence. While he'd obviously seen to the house, gardening didn't appear to be Captain Bill's strong suit. She heard the sound again and placed it as coming from the barn. *Of course! Captain Bill!* He hadn't said he'd be here to greet her. Instead, he'd indicated he'd leave the door unlocked and she could let herself in. No one locked anything in these parts, according to Captain Bill. Still, Melissa had insisted as part of their arrangement that he'd provide her with a key. His creaky old voice had rattled back to her through the telephone. *If I can find it.*

When Melissa had telephoned to rent this property, she'd learned that Captain Bill had run a deep-sea fishing operation for many years. He'd led charters out from Port Scarborough, the nearby harbor town, and into the Atlantic Ocean by way of the Chesapeake Bay. Now, he'd retired from that and mostly spent his days looking after this place and others like it, where the owners lived out of state and rented the properties to vacationers during the summer months. Melissa had heard of the Virginia Eastern Shore from a couple of colleagues who regularly vacationed here from New

York. She'd been seeking someplace near the water, yet quiet and undisturbed. They'd assured her the area surrounding Port Scarborough would fit the bill.

Melissa exited by the back door, crossing through the screened porch that housed cushioned wicker furniture. It would be a lovely spot to sit and enjoy her morning coffee while gazing out at the cove, provided mornings here weren't too cold. Melissa raised the zipper on her jacket to combat a biting chill as she strode toward the barn, autumn grass crunching beneath her boots. When she rounded the corner to the barn's front door, she spied first the bumper of a truck and then the whole thing. It was a beat-up blue Chevy from at least a few decades back. Maybe more than a few. *Yep, has to be the captain.* She approached the barn door, finding it partially ajar. The clanking grew louder. "Hello!" Melissa called above the racket. "Captain—?" Melissa spied a lean figure crouched over a mower and abruptly stopped. This certainly wasn't the older gentleman she'd expected. A hunky younger man with stunning gray eyes looked up at her, and Melissa felt a lightning bolt of recognition. But that was impossible. She'd clearly never seen this guy before. He appeared to be around her age, perhaps a few years older.

Stone Thomas stopped hammering the metal blade of the mower with his wrench and stared at the woman who'd just entered the barn. For a moment he thought his eyes were playing tricks on him. Then he hoped to goodness they weren't. There, in the open barn door, stood the most engagingly beautiful woman Stone had encountered in years. Maybe ever. Honey-blond hair cascaded past her shoulders as she gazed at him with big blue eyes set in an angelic face. She couldn't have stood much over five feet and packed what was apparently a dynamite figure into black stretch jeans. Her knee-high boots matched the worn appearance of her brushed leather jacket, which was zipped all the way up beneath a white winter scarf. Stone's pulse pounded and then his heart beat faster as she trapped him in an inquiring gaze. "Well, howdy," he said, straightening to greet her.

"Captain...Bill?" she asked weakly. Was it Stone's imagination or did a hint of color sweep her cheeks?

"Hardly that," he said. "But give me a few years and you might mistake us for twins." He shot her a grin, but she didn't take the bait. Instead, she just blinked at him like she'd seen a ghost. Stone dusted his palms against his jeans to wipe off any grime, feeling foolish. "Sorry about that. I guess I didn't miss my calling as a stand-up comedian." He extended a hand. "Stone Thomas." The woman eyed him warily, but held her ground.

"Is the captain around?" she asked coolly. "He said he might stop by, but didn't mention anyone else being here."

Stone dropped his hand, which had been dangling in midair, and slid it into his jeans pocket. "He said to tell you he'll come by tomorrow."

"Tomorrow?" she asked with dismay. "But he promised to—"

"Bring you this?" Stone pulled the key from his pocket and held it toward her, palm up. "You're lucky he found it. I don't think anyone's used it in years."

She tentatively inched forward and took the key from him. "Thanks," she said, forcing a little smile. She appeared to be viewing him oddly, surveying his face. What had Stone forgotten to do? Shave this morning?

He rubbed his scratchy chin, realizing that ritual had slipped his mind.

The woman motioned toward the John Deere riding mower that he'd laid on its side. "Is that where all the clanking was coming from?"

Stone shrugged and displayed his wrench. "It's got a bent blade. I was aiming to fix it, before putting it up for the winter."

"You...work here?" she asked on a tentative breath that clouded the air. The temperatures had taken a dip and now hovered just above freezing. Stone had shut off the outdoor taps in preparation for the first frost of the season.

"I keep things tidy around the yard." His eyes settled on hers. "It's an awfully big one."

Melissa felt herself color again in spite of herself. The guy was over six feet tall and extremely handsome in a rough-hewn way, with a chiseled face and a manly jaw.

"That's what I gather." She hesitated, then asked, her brow raised, "Are you about finished?"

Stone pressed his lips together to keep from chuckling. "Almost done. I'm sorry if the racket disturbed you. I honestly didn't know you were here. The captain said you weren't expected till later this evening."

"Of course." She exhaled softly, feeling more at ease in his company. Naturally, she'd surprised Stone just as much as he'd surprised her. "Now it's my turn to apologize for showing up early."

"No need. The house is yours for a month, I hear."

"At least."

"You planning on buying?"

"Beg pardon?" she asked.

Stone carefully surveyed her. "You *did* know it's for sale?"

Melissa wasn't sure she liked the sound of this. She'd come here expecting solitude, not a barrage of realtors and prospective buyers traipsing through her rental home. "You mean that while I'm here, agents will be—?"

Stone shook his head. "Nothing like that. Fact is, I don't believe anyone's come to see it in..." He scratched his head as if remembering. "Well, not in a very long time."

"Is there something wrong with the house?" she asked quietly.

"That place?" He motioned with his wrench through the open barn door. "Not a thing. It's as grand as they come. Might even buy it myself one day."

"I see." He caught her eyes on the wrench and gingerly set it down beside him on a bound bale of hay.

Melissa suddenly felt silly for acting standoffish. Stone had been nothing but cordial and she'd blatantly blown off his initial greeting. "I'm sorry if I was rude earlier."

"Rude?"

"When you introduced yourself."

A smile tickled his lips. "I'd never blame a lady for being cautious. Particularly when she comes across the likes of me."

Melissa's eyes did a quick sweep of Stone's muscled chest and arms. A field jacket hung across the back of a sawhorse beside him. He'd obviously removed the jacket and rolled up his flannel shirt's sleeves to tackle the job with the mower. Stone was well built and looked like he was used to working with his hands. His dark brown hair was cut short and stubble covered his chin.

"When I didn't take your hand, I didn't mean to imply—"

"No implications taken," he said graciously. Soulful gray eyes met hers. They reminded her of a storm at the ocean. "Don't sweat it."

Even as he said it, she broiled with heat beneath her snug leather jacket. Stone was incredibly handsome, and unless he owned a ring but never wore it, he was also single. And single men were just one of the things Melissa had come here to get away from. Particularly drop-dead gorgeous single men who spoke with a slight Southside Virginia southern twang. She spoke past the lump in her throat. "Thanks for bringing by the key."

"You be sure to lock up tight now," he said, teasing her. Mischief danced in his eyes and Melissa felt dizzy from Stone's perusal. "I will. And, by the way," she added a bit breathlessly, "my name's Melissa."

A slow grin spread across his gorgeous face. "Just Melissa?"

Melissa's cheeks flamed. "Carter!" she spouted quickly, before backing away. Then she spun around and hurried toward the house before she could think or do anything foolish, such as ask Stone more about himself. Like where he lived, or how often he'd be around.

Not that she cared if Stone came by. If he'd been hired to help oversee the place, who was she to stand in the way? As long as he kept himself outdoors, things would be fine. Besides, how much tending could the lawn really need at this time of year? Melissa decided she could always ask Captain Bill about this tomorrow and put her mind at ease. Since she'd come to work at

Homecoming Cove, she couldn't have folks showing up unexpectedly. If the captain could supply some sort of maintenance schedule, that would help.

Melissa entered the house, then busied herself with carrying groceries and luggage in from her SUV. She became so focused on her task, she nearly forgot about the handsome man in the barn—until his truck rumbled past her on the gravel drive as she carted in her final load. Melissa turned on the stoop to wave good-bye, and Stone sent her a mock captain's salute from inside the cab. A giggle escaped her, then Melissa stopped and caught her breath. In a very weird way, she had the sense that she'd experienced that exchange with Stone before.

Melissa stood there, her heart pounding, as Stone's truck drove away. His actions must have recalled her to an earlier time, something she couldn't quite place. Or maybe she was just feeling giddy because a good-looking guy had smiled in her direction. Not that she'd been encouraging smiles from eligible men lately. Most often, she turned and looked the other way. Peter had definitely messed with her head, and she needed time to get it together. She hoped this working vacation at the Virginia Eastern Shore would provide the opportunity for that.

Chapter Two

After she'd stowed her provisions away, Melissa opened a jar of homemade spaghetti sauce and dumped it in a pot, setting the burner to simmer. Last summer she'd put up two dozen jars of sauce made with fresh produce gathered from a farmers' market, and she had slowly been working her way through them. Melissa filled a pasta pot with water and placed it on the stove to boil, eager to explore the rest of the house. She'd opted to start supper first, as she was famished. Melissa hadn't eaten anything since the meager cheese sandwich she'd packed for the road, and it had been a long drive from New York to Virginia.

The Chesapeake Bay Bridge Tunnel had plummeted her SUV into a deep underwater tube, then sent her zooming skyward onto a snaking expanse of bridge that seemed to go on forever. It felt almost like being on a roller coaster, only she'd been moving much more slowly. Melissa could imagine the backups that must occur along this lone route to Chincoteague and other environs in peak summer months. But in October, things were quieter and she'd fortunately hit very little traffic heading this way. Seagulls had dived for the waves around her and she'd lowered her windows to catch a whiff of the crisp salty air. This getaway was just what she needed. Plus, it would give her an opportunity to work.

Once satisfied that her meal preparations were on track, Melissa walked to the foyer and hoisted her two heavy bags off the floor. According to her online research, the weather was a bit unpredictable here this time of year, so she'd packed a variety of clothing ranging from shorts, T-shirts, and tennis shoes to jeans, sweaters, and boots. Only just this afternoon she'd been grateful for her winter scarf and glad that she'd brought her gloves and hat as well. The wind was bitterly fierce when it ripped off the water, even in this mostly protected inlet.

As she hadn't spotted it before, she guessed the staircase leading to the second story was through the parlor on the far side of the dining room. Night had settled in, so Melissa paused to switch lights on as she went along. When she reached the parlor, she set down both bags with a satisfied sigh. A glorious antique upright piano stood against the left wall near the center of the room and beside a front-facing window. Beyond the next doorway, Melissa spied a small hall and a staircase tucked inside it. With the exception of the kitchen, which connected to the foyer containing the front door, each room on the main floor spanned the width of the house, affording views of both the oak-lined drive out front and the expansive back lawn. Melissa could only imagine what a glorious room the parlor must be when it was completely filled with sunlight.

Melissa approached the piano as if it were a living thing and carefully slid back the dust cover concealing the keyboard. The ivories glimmered in the pale lamplight, inviting her touch. She trilled off a series of notes, each one ringing clear and harmonious. How lucky that the piano was in tune.

Melissa peeked out a darkened window next to the piano at the front lawn. Next, she turned around completely to view the shadowy cove through the room's other window, which was positioned opposite the piano. It framed the run-down garden she'd seen earlier, which sat on this side of the barn and was surrounded by a white picket fence. Beyond the fence sat the footpath that led across the grassy expanse hedging the water and then downhill to the small private beach. The back of the house had an eastern exposure, meaning Melissa could sit at the piano and work while being bathed from behind in morning sunlight. It was the ideal location to get her career back on track, the career that had taken a sudden nosedive after Melissa's recent romantic disaster.

Melissa wrote musical themes for a number of popular television shows and made-for-cable movies. At times her compositions were dramatic and hinted at danger; at others, they were jovial and light. Some were ponderous, and a few were sweepingly romantic. She was given a working copy of the script with director's notes for where the music fit in. The final renditions were very rarely played on a piano, but once she'd delivered her part, it was up to others in production to decide on execution. It was really quite interesting work, and it paid very well. Except for during those times when Melissa got stuck due to her inability to create, she thought sourly, lifting her suitcases.

Melissa frowned and trudged up the stairs, embarrassed by her failings as a professional. In more than ten years of contract work she'd never been unable to complete an assignment until now. But since her falling-out with Peter, she'd felt totally blocked. She'd been ashamed to ask the current production team for an extension on her present assignment. Melissa had never needed to do that before, and she wasn't proud that she'd missed a deadline. Fortunately, everyone in charge had been very understanding and had agreed to grant her another month. The fact that the lead actress's pregnancy had delayed the production schedule had helped buy Melissa time.

Melissa reached the upstairs landing and snapped to attention. The water pot she'd left on the stove might be boiling over by now. She'd need to hurry things along. Melissa stole a quick glance through the open doors of three cozily decorated bedrooms, locating the master. It was situated to the rear of the house, overlooking the cove, and was double the size of the other two bedrooms across the hall. It was also the only room with its own bath. The other two shared a Jack-and-Jill bathroom between them. Not everything in this house was original. The plumbing and totally renovated kitchen had obviously been added later. Melissa set her suitcases on the queen-size bed, pleased to see that this room also had an eastern exposure. The two large windows bookending the headboard would provide a stunning morning panorama of Homecoming Cove. But at the moment, there was supper to fix. Melissa's stomach rumbled as if urging her along.

She'd barely returned to the kitchen when the large pot started bubbling fiercely. Melissa turned down the flame on the gas burner and gingerly added a fistful of pasta, tossing in a few strands of spaghetti at a time. The sauce was already simmering in the small saucepan nearby. All Melissa needed to complete her meal was wine. She reached for a bottle of Chianti in the wine rack she'd stocked and found a corkscrew in the drawer by the sink. Once she'd poured herself a glass and recorked the bottle, Melissa looked out through the window. The shadowy dock was threaded with moonlight as an opaque quarter moon rose over the water, and the barn stood in the swaying gloom of the trees.

Melissa found herself thinking of Stone and her odd déjà vu moment on the stoop. It wasn't only then, either. She'd experienced a flash of recognition when she'd first seen him in the barn as well. When Stone had turned his eyes on hers, it had been almost like meeting an old friend. But that was ridiculous, surely. There was no way she and Stone ever could have met. Stone seemed like a local, and Melissa had spent her entire life in New York. Melissa took a thoughtful sip of wine, supposing she might have passed someone resembling Stone on the subway, or on a bustling New York City street. It wasn't uncommon for one person to look like another, and there were certainly a lot of people in New York. In fact, the odds of someone there looking like Stone were probably pretty high. Heat rose in Melissa's cheeks when the blatant fact struck her: very few men were as good-looking as Stone. If Melissa had spied someone like him before, even in passing, she definitely would have remembered. Stone had a rugged appearance that would have made him stand out among the well-polished men of New York.

The beeper went off and Melissa realized she'd been lost in her reverie for more than ten minutes. She went to tend to the pasta, but when she carried the full pot toward the colander she'd placed in the sink, Melissa's gaze snagged on a spot above the kitchen window. Though she hadn't seen it before, she now

clearly viewed the heartwarming sign. It was cheerily
painted with pretty rosebud illustrations surrounding its
stenciled words. Its colors were faded, as if the piece of
painted wood had been hanging over the kitchen
window for a very long time. Melissa dumped her pasta
into the colander, then backed away from the burst of
steam to once again observe the message. While it was
probably nothing more than a gracious welcome, the
sentiment seemed poignant somehow.

*May those who come together here, never fall
apart.*

Melissa stared out the window toward the water,
then her eyes felt pulled to the white picket fence
surrounding the dilapidated garden. She thought again
of Stone and her eerie déjà vu. She'd felt it with him—
not just once, but two times—and in such a short span
of time. A sudden chill enveloped her, but she shook it
off with another sip of wine. Melissa had heard of
instant attraction, and believed that some people felt an
unexplained connection with each other. But that
certainly wasn't going on between her and Stone. For
all she knew, these feelings were all one-sided.
Desperately one-sided, Melissa thought with chagrin.

*This is what I get for swearing off dating. A hot guy
says "howdy," and my imagination runs wild.* "Supper
time," she told herself, grabbing a plate from the
counter. Then she heaped it full of spaghetti and sauce
and carried it and her wine into the dining room.

Tonight, after tidying up the kitchen, she'd tuck
herself into bed early with a good book. Tomorrow,
she'd forget all about the hot groundskeeper and foolish
notions—and get to work.

Chapter Three

Stone tossed and turned, trying to get his bearings.
He was on board ship again, crewing another sailboat in
the Caribbean. The winds were high and the sea
chopped in big, angry waves. He'd picked up this line
of work after hearing about it from a friend. You got
paid to sail all day among some of the most beautiful
islands in the world. All you had to do was keep the big
boat steady for the wealthy city slickers who longed for
adventure, but didn't want to sweat for it. This morning
Stone had gotten into an argument with the captain over
the weather, and now the captain admitted he'd made a
mistake. They should never have ventured into deep
waters with a tropical storm brewing. Stone had called
it from the pink cast on the horizon mixed with
threatening dark clouds. The captain had believed it a
passing storm in the distance and thought it was
blowing farther out to sea. Now, in a matter of minutes
it would be fully upon them. Stone just hoped they'd
have to time make port.

Thunder boomed and gales gusted as a woman
shrieked in her cabin below. There were three couples
on board and a cook, plus the captain and Stone, who
skippered the boat. Unfortunately for everyone today,
Stone hadn't been the man in charge. Five minutes

before, when the heavy rains started pounding the deck, the captain had ordered everyone else below and into their life jackets. Stone tugged the belt of his vest tighter, cinching it against his six-pack. Crewing boats had left him muscled and tanned, but he still wasn't happy in the water. He'd always had an irrational fear of it, no matter how much he'd trained himself as an expert swimmer with a diving certification. There was one thing Stone understood about nature: you had to respect its enormous power.

The ocean rose in swells around them, slamming first the starboard and then the port side of the boat with tremendous force. Stone lowered the main sail and secured its sheets, then went after the spinnaker. Squinting through the downpour, he could see the captain wrestling with the tiller. Stone had a horrific premonition seconds before the boat came around, making a rapid about-face. More screams echoed from below as the boat keeled sideways and torrents of seawater flooded the deck. One of the husbands yelled some kind of curse just as Stone saw the boom swinging toward him, the lines meant to secure it whipping frenetically behind it in the wind. Before he had time to duck, Stone was dealt a blow to his shoulder, rocketing him overboard.

Stone sat up in bed in a panicked sweat. His brow was sopping wet and his T-shirt was soaked. He tried to breathe, but he couldn't. He was drowning…*drowning,* sinking farther and farther into the ocean's abyss. Stone rested his head in his hands and drew a deep choking breath, and then another. The air wheezed through his lungs and he gasped, his chest heaving. At last the moment passed, and his pulse slowed as he took in his surroundings. Moonlight angled through the panes of his rustic cabin's windows and danced across the pine floor. *It was a dream*, he told himself. *But not just any dream:* the *dream.* He'd had drowning dreams since he was eight years old. When he was a child, it was a large wave that would overtake him while he was bodysurfing and drag him into the undertow. The current was always too strong and impossible to fight.

Over the years, the dream had taken on different incarnations, but the outcome was always the same. After the episode in the Caribbean, which everyone fortunately survived, Stone had become plagued by that setting in his more recent nightmares. Despite his close call in getting thrown overboard, he had been credited by the captain with saving the ship. His fast thinking during the storm had kept everyone belowdecks safe, and before he'd been tossed out to sea Stone had had the presence of mind to clip an additional line between his harness and one of the cleats on the deck in case the standard jackline failed to hold him. That backup line had been used by the captain to pull Stone out of the water—and save his life. But no matter what kind of hero the rest of the people on that boat tried to make Stone out to be, he decided he'd had enough. Enough of sailing and enough of being on the water. Yet, he couldn't run away from it completely. Stone came from generations of men who'd worked the seas. The ocean was in his blood.

When Stone had moved back to Port Scarborough, he was seeking a more peaceful existence. But his skill set was limited to what he could do with his hands. Since Stone knew boats, his grandpa suggested he apply for a job at a local business, repairing motors and patching damaged hulls. It was solid work and it got him by, but it didn't alleviate that tug in his soul. That secret voice that told him there was something else he was meant to do. Stone turned toward the window, thinking he'd heard music. A light, melodious sound like the tinkling of keys.

Tossing aside the covers, Stone padded barefoot toward the front door. The modest cabin was a one-room affair with a tiny galley kitchen and an even smaller bathroom barely accommodating a toilet, sink, and shower. But it had a nice woodstove to keep him warm in winter, and he couldn't beat the rent. His grandpa had offered it to him for free in exchange for groundskeeping at the House at Homecoming Cove. The fifty-acre parcel was way more than an old man could keep up. So Stone took care of the grunt work of cutting back the fields and routinely clearing the land, while maintaining the lawn around the main house. "Captain Bill" took care of any handyman-type tinkering that needed doing.

Stone opened the cabin's door and stepped out onto its covered porch, tracking the sound through the night. Far away and beyond the trees he spied a glimmer of light as the music continued. Stone checked the angle of the moon, guessing it had to be after three in the morning. Apparently, Melissa Carter was some kind of musical insomniac. But, she was a talented one. There was no denying that. The melody was light and sweet, almost whimsical, like a child's lullaby designed to enchant an innocent heart. His own ticker couldn't resist the tug of it. The tune was soothing like the ocean's sound, swelling and falling in lulling waves.

Stone reflected on this, thinking he'd never actually heard that piano played. It was one of the few pieces of furniture that was original to the house, and it sounded mysteriously well-tuned after having sat idle all this time. Stone cocked his ear to the wind and listened a few minutes more, trying to envision Melissa seated at the piano, her delicately boned hands moving deftly across the keys. Was her hair tied up, or sexily undone, the way it had been this afternoon in the barn? The music crescendoed and a sea-storm of emotion rose within him. Her playing was every bit as beautiful as she was. Not that a sophisticated woman like Melissa would take an interest in a man like him. Someone who was still painfully getting his act together. The breeze picked up, drowning out the final chords of her song. Then, when the wind died down again, all was still, with only a hoot owl calling in the distance.

Chapter Four

Melissa rose cheerily from her bed the next day, feeling better rested than she'd been in months. She stared out her bedroom window, seeing that the sun was up and the sky burned bright blue. Fall foliage fluttered around the edges of the cove, tree limbs curtseying in the breeze. She couldn't wait to pour some coffee and sit on the screened porch to enjoy the morning. Her pajama pants were probably warm enough, but the meager T-shirt wouldn't do. Melissa reached into the wardrobe and pulled out a big nubby sweater. It was way oversized and likely the most comfortable item of clothing she owned. She slipped it on, then fluffed her hair before heading downstairs, delighted to have so few things on her agenda.

Back home, her computer would be blaring with new alerts and her cell would be buzzing with messages. Out here, at Homecoming Cove, there wasn't even cell service. No Internet either. Just lots and lots of water and land. Melissa had still brought her laptop so she could add her compositions to her music-writing program, once she'd perfected them by ear first and written them down on the spiral-bound pad of music paper. For her, composing was a three-part invention, and she was excited to think about how smoothly that process might go without all the routine distractions.

The view from the kitchen window was just as lovely as Melissa recalled from yesterday. She smiled to herself and poured some coffee from the pot she'd set to auto-brew last night. As she exited onto the porch, the nip in the air was sharp but not unbearable. There was a throw blanket folded over the back of one chair she could use to warm her legs. She tucked them up under herself and settled into the wicker love seat with her coffee. Melissa took a welcome sip from her mug, savoring her surroundings. A fine mist lifted off the water, emitting a hazy glow in the warming sun. Birds chirped and gulls called, sailing above the cove. There was no better place to be at this moment in time.

Melissa sighed, wondering what it would be like to live in a historic farmhouse like this forever. Its weathered beauty was romantic, but she also guessed taking care of it would involve substantial work. She recalled what Stone had said about the place being for sale, and wondered curiously why no one had bought it. It was certainly a cool house and extensive renovations had been made. Plus, the setting was dramatic. Still, it was fairly far from anything. *No, make that very far from everything!*

Melissa smiled over the rim of her mug, thinking that was what made it perfect. There was not another soul around, besides Captain Bill, whom she'd yet to meet, and, oh yeah…*Stone.* Melissa's cheeks warmed at the recollection of his name. When she'd counted herself lucky for Homecoming Cove's lack of distractions, she'd failed to consider him. Part of her hoped the good-looking groundskeeper wouldn't be around that much. But then her other half hoped that he would. There was something in his sultry gray eyes that made her heart thunder and her insides melt like chocolate…exquisite Swiss chocolate with a low melting point. Melissa recalled Stone's sexy smile and a slow burn moved through her, igniting regions she'd believed permanently doused in ice.

Melissa downed the last of her coffee, shocked by where her thoughts were going. She was here to compose, not to become involved with some local man. Not that Stone Thomas would be interested in the least. Which was fine, because she wasn't either. Peter had caused her to question many things: not just where she'd been, but also where she was going. And Melissa had decided she wanted the journey to be totally up to her. She didn't need someone like Peter to validate her. He'd actually done her a favor by revealing his true character before she and he had become more deeply involved. Still, his words had stung her deeply. So deeply, she'd feared for a time she might not be able to move forward.

Fortunately, Melissa was a strong woman and she ultimately realized that she would get past this. Melissa wouldn't apologize for herself or her family. She was proud of who she was, and where she'd come from. At the end of the day, it really was Peter's loss.

Chapter Five

Later that morning, Melissa sat at the antique piano composing her second song of the day. She'd already knocked out the first piece in record time. It was astounding. The moment she'd set her hands on the keys, her creativity had blossomed, almost like a bouquet of rosebuds blooming in the sunshine. As stunning as it seemed, it was as if the piano led her, and not the other way around. The well-seasoned instrument seemed to sense her every mood, anticipate each turn of her wrist and the approach of her nimble fingers. Chords heightened, then fell, leading seamlessly into the next.

She was writing a melody for a made-for-cable movie, a heartfelt love story about former high-school sweethearts returning to their hometown and finding each other once again. How fitting it was that Melissa felt so at home here, in this random Virginia farmhouse so far from the rest of the world.

Melissa closed her eyes and let the fingers of her left hand tumble gracefully down an octave, as her right hand expertly commanded a lilting trill. There was no effort to her playing, only ease. And to think she'd been blocked for so long, unable to compose even a few simple bars.

"Well, I'll be," an old man's voice suddenly intruded. "Aren't you the spitting image of—?"

Melissa's eyes popped open and she shrieked, spinning abruptly on the bench. "Captain Bill?" she asked, aghast.

He stood there dressed in overalls and an old hunting jacket. The wavy white hair on his head matched his fisherman's mustache and beard. He held a plaid tam in one hand and a pair of work gloves in the other. He clutched an unlit pipe in his teeth and spoke around it. "That's right," he said unapologetically. "You must be Melissa."

"You scared me half to death," she told him honestly. "You might have knocked."

"Did." He shoved the work gloves in his pocket and withdrew a packet of loose tobacco. "Ya didn't hear me."

Melissa tucked an errant strand of hair behind one ear, gathering her composure. She'd thought to lock the front door, but must have mistakenly left the door leading to the back porch unlocked after partaking of her morning coffee.

He stared at her a long while before speaking again. "Hear tell you met my grandson."

"Grand…?" The realization hit her. "Stone? Oh, why yes. Yes, I did. He was very kind to give me the key."

"Don't think you'll need it."

She smiled politely. "Maybe I should be the judge of that."

Captain Bill grunted, then said, "Suit yourself." He carefully filled his pipe bowl with tobacco and tamped it down. As he did, Melissa could have sworn she heard him grumble, *"City woman."*

"I'd appreciate it if you didn't smoke in here." She stood, attempting to herd him toward the porch. Captain Bill eyed her over the flame of the match he'd just lit and shook it out. "I beg your pardon," he said with an exaggerated degree of contrition. "Not used to having too many folks around here. 'Specially not *lady folks*."

He turned casually and made his way through the kitchen and the living room and onto the porch. Melissa followed him in a haze of disbelief and disapproval. *The man just walks right in, and doesn't even apologize! To top it off he wants to smoke indoors?*

"Captain Bill," she told him calmly when they reached the porch. "I appreciate your coming by to check on me, but I'm all settled in."

Failing to get the hint, he took a seat on a wicker chair. "That's good to hear." He took his time lighting his pipe and took a deep drag. "No problems, then?" he asked through a puff of gray smoke.

"None that I've noticed." Melissa sat on a neighboring chair, understanding this was going to take a while. Captain Bill apparently wasn't leaving until he'd had his smoke. "The house was in very good order when I arrived. Immaculate. Thank you."

He met her gaze with light blue eyes and something in his countenance reminded Melissa of Stone. While Bill's face was older and more weather-worn than Stone's, their features held a certain resemblance, particularly around the jawline. "Good to know you're pleased. Stone said you would be."

"Oh?" she asked, surprised.

"Said he could tell this was the place for you. You and your musical abilities."

"Musical? I don't understand."

"Play piano, don't you?" Bill said matter-of-factly. "Now, you can go on and deny it, but I caught ya red-handed, right in there." He motioned behind him with his pipe.

"I'm not denying anything," Melissa replied, feeling out of sorts. "I'm just not getting how Stone could have possibly known."

Bill shot her an ominous stare. "Boy's clairvoyant."

"What?"

No sooner had she responded than a chuckle burst out of his lips. "Sorry, missy," Bill said, shaking his head. "Couldn't resist it. Truth is, I told him you asked about the piano when you rented. 'Bout how you insisted the house had to have a working one before you'd take it." He eyed her thoughtfully for a few moments more. "Getting spooked being here, are ya?"

"Spooked? No. Why would I be?"

"'Cause of the legend, you know."

Captain Bill was obviously teasing her, just as Stone had enjoyed razzing her about the key. Perhaps it was a family trait. "No, I don't know," she said mildly. "Maybe you could enlighten me?"

"Don't want to give you any nightmares."

"I don't have nightmares," Melissa said evenly. "In fact, I rarely dream."

"Everyone dreams every night," Captain Bill assured her. "In your case, you probably just don't remember."

Melissa raised both eyebrows. *My, isn't he a know-it-all.* "Well, if you don't want to tell me…" she said, starting to stand.

"Hold your horses and sit back down."

She shot him a steely look.

"If you please," he said with some humility. "The story won't take long."

Melissa settled back in her seat, mildly interested. She didn't really believe in ghosts, but she did like reading about them. Besides, if this house was reputed to be haunted, what a fantastic story she'd have to tell her friends when she returned to New York. *I stayed in this really cool place on Virginia's Eastern Shore, and it was—*

"It all started with Fiona," Captain Bill said, cutting off her thoughts.

"Fiona?"

"The beautiful young woman who owned this place."

"How long ago was this?"

"Turn of the century. The last one. Early nineteen hundreds."

"What happened to her?"

"It's a very sad story. Fiona was engaged to Lewis, a strapping young man and a sea captain. Ran fishing boats out of Port Scarborough just up the way. Rumor holds the two of them loved each other very much and vowed to stay together." Captain Bill reached for a coffee can on an end table and dumped his tobacco ash into it, then he knocked his pipe against the sole of his shoe and shook it out again. "Lewis went out to sea one cold winter's day." Bill gazed out at the cove, his expression melancholy. "He never came back again."

"How tragic."

"Sure was. Particularly for his betrothed, Fiona."

"They weren't married?"

"They'd planned to wed in February. This house was part of Fiona's dowry. Her father built it for the young couple to live in. Unfortunately, they never got the chance."

"What happened to Fiona?" Melissa asked softly.

"Died shortly after Lewis's boat was lost at sea. Some say it was of a broken heart. Others claim it was the pneumonia that took her. She spent day after day on that icy pier…through wind, rain, and snow…just waiting for her true love to return."

Melissa followed his gaze out onto the water. "How sad for the two of them. Well, at least they're finally together."

"Yep, there's that." Bill tucked his pipe in his pocket and stood. "Anyway," he said, his heavy mood lifting. "That's the story of Lewis and Fiona, and why nobody will buy this place."

"Because two people connected to it died? So long ago?" Melissa blinked at him. "That doesn't make sense."

"Not to you or me, maybe it doesn't. But around Port Scarborough, the story's gotten bigger. You'd be surprised by how superstitious people can get. And some of 'em got whoppers of imaginations. Even claim to have heard the piano playing here while anchored at Homecoming Cove."

"Well, maybe they—"

"I mean, when nobody was home."

Melissa felt a chill race down her spine. But that was silly, wasn't it? The house was old, sure. But it was also warm and welcoming. Hadn't she felt comfortable here ever since walking in? And just look at how her music had flourished, and all within the course of one day. "I guess you just can't figure people out," she finally said.

"No."

"Well, obviously Stone doesn't believe in those stories," Melissa added, remembering his comment. "He said he might buy the property."

Captain Bill smiled fondly. "The boy very well might…someday."

"Who owns the house now?" Melissa asked him.

"Family up in Boston, the Brandons. Massachusetts stock. The older generation were whalers up there off of Nantucket. Made a fortune, but didn't like the winters. Bought this place as a holiday retreat."

"But it snows down here."

"Not like it does up there. And anyways, they liked the lay of the land, as well as them wild ponies up the road."

"What made them decide to sell?"

"The younger generation don't use it. They've got other houses bigger than this. So they decided to fix this one up even better, with a spanking new kitchen and bathrooms, thinking they'd offload it."

"But no nibbles?"

"Bad fishing," Captain Bill said with a grin. "They want too much for it, and when big-money prospective buyers start nosing around, the townsfolk are all too happy to jump in with their scary stories. Think they'd rather it sold to somebody local, not that anyone around here's got that kind of cash. Well, almost nobody…" he said, stopping himself. "Anyways, Melissa. This old man's bored you long enough." He nodded and his blue eyes sparkled. "Just give a holler if you need anything, or discover anything amiss. My number's on the card right by the kitchen phone."

Unexpectedly, Melissa felt sorry to see him go. To her astonishment, she was actually starting to enjoy his company. As irascible as he was, Captain Bill had his own unique charm. "Thanks again for stopping by, Captain Bill, and for sharing your story."

"Anytime," he said, setting his cap on his head.

It was then that she remembered to ask about Stone.

"Captain Bill!" she called before he could let himself out the screen door that led to the patio. "I meant to ask about Stone."

"Yeah? What about him?"

"What I mean is, I was wondering when I might expect him?"

Captain Bill eyed her uncertainly. "If you'd like him to come by I can—"

"No! It's not that I'd *like him to*. What I mean is... Of course, that would be fine. I mean, if he needs to." Melissa drew a rushed breath. "I guess what I'm asking is whether he has any sort of schedule?"

"Schedule?"

"For groundskeeping."

"He don't generally clock in and out, if that's what you're asking." He cocked his head to the side, repressing a grin. "But I'll tell him you asked after him."

"Oh, no." Melissa bit her bottom lip. "That won't be necessary."

Captain Bill clucked his tongue. "Whatever you'd like."

"So, he doesn't then?"

"Doesn't what?" Captain Bill asked, befuddled.

"Have any set—?"

"Heavens to Betsy, girl!" Bill snapped with feigned annoyance. "See those leaves up there? When those come down, he'll be round to rake them. Might be here to clean out the gutters too. Want any more specifics than that, I'm afraid you'll have to take it up with Stone himself."

Melissa swallowed hard, feeling like a chastised schoolgirl. "No problem."

"Good," he said gruffly, walking away. "Don't forget about my number!"

When he was halfway to his truck, Melissa stopped him again. "Captain Bill?"

He slowly turned her way as wind rustled through the trees.

"Just one more thing. When you surprised me in the house, you said something. Something about me looking like someone? Who exactly were you referring to?"

Bill studied the ground a lingering moment and adjusted his cap. "Why, the young woman I was just telling you about." He met her eyes and she knew by instinct what he was about to say. "Fiona."

Chapter Six

Melissa paced back and forth behind the old piano, unable to sit…unwilling to write. She had the final chords from a tune knocking around in her head, but felt disinclined to jot them down. She felt restless and uneasy, her thoughts repeatedly returning to poor Fiona and her heartbreaking tale. Though she shouldn't have let it unnerve her, Melissa had been oddly unsettled by Captain Bill's assertion that she looked like Fiona. Then again, people often mistook her for someone else, especially in New York. Perhaps her blond-haired, blue-eyed appearance was more universal than she liked to think.

Melissa surveyed the piano, one of the few original pieces of furniture that had remained in this house, and wondered whether it had once been played by Fiona. Melissa tried to envision Fiona being in this room with her hands on the keys, and a shiver tore through her.

A sharp breeze came out of nowhere, and Melissa jerked her head around toward the window framing the cove. Beside it, a gauzy white curtain billowed in a trembling column, as if a person were cloaked underneath it. Melissa stood there transfixed, her rational mind battling her fear.

The sheer fabric swelled and shimmied, softly swaying this way and that. Melissa's blood pumped harder and she opened her mouth to scream. Then her eye snagged on the heat register on the floor below the window, and she realized it had begun cranking out air. Of course—it was the heat! What had she been thinking? Too much about dead people and days gone by, Melissa decided, releasing a shuddering breath.

She stared through the window, observing the blustery day outdoors. While the sun had risen higher, the temperature had seemed to drop with each passing hour. But Melissa didn't mind the cold, especially as she'd come prepared to dress for it. Maybe what she needed was a break to freshen her perspective. A brisk walk in the country might help.

Stone stood on the small dock, a rod in hand and his tackle box by his feet. He was trout fishing in the private pond that sat near his cabin on the grounds. He didn't know why the fish weren't biting today, but he decided to give them another chance. After rebaiting his hook, he made a skillful cast, sending the tackle arching skyward before it plummeted toward the water and sank gracefully below the surface. The wealthy owners of this place, the Brandons, saw fit to periodically restock this freshwater pond, in the event someone in their family might want to make use of it. But in the eight months Stone had served as groundskeeper, he'd only seen members of that clan fish from it twice.

While the Brandons may have descended from whalers, there didn't appear to be much true fisherman's blood left in many of them. Perhaps that was in part why they were selling this farm. The owners scarcely visited, and seldom took advantage of the area's local wonders when they did. Mostly, they seemed inclined to sit on the porch and sip fancy-looking drinks from chilled highball glasses. Since that meant better fishing for him, that was A-OK with Stone. With the Brandons' permission, he could keep all of his catch from both the pond and the creek, which contained its own healthy supply of delicious Virginia blue crab. Stone was likewise free to take out any of the house's kayaks, rowboats, or canoes, though he rarely did the latter. Now that Stone was off of the water, he was happy to stay off, thank you very much.

Stone looked up, thinking he'd heard rustling through the trees. It sounded like something was approaching along the footpath leading from the main house. He peered in that direction, spying a pair of antlers poking out from behind the brush. The entire buck emerged and the handsome white-tailed deer turned toward him, his gaze defiantly fixed on Stone's. Then suddenly, he skittered forward as if spooked, before wheeling back around on prancing hooves and galloping toward a neighboring thicket.

Melissa froze by a bayberry bush as the enormous animal thundered past her, nearly knocking her off her feet. The huge buck wound its way toward the water, then was lost in a gnarly tangle of underbrush, the tip of its white tail flicking madly. Melissa startled initially, then released a peal of laughter. She was silly to be afraid. The poor creature was likely much more terrified of her—or by whatever it had encountered in that clearing up ahead. Melissa cautiously tiptoed toward it, unsure of what she might find. Another display of wildlife?

Melissa reached the end of the footpath and her heart stilled. A honey-colored field opened up before her, with tall shafts of wheat waving beyond it. A homey-looking cabin sat to one side, smoke curling from a pipe in its tin roof. And to the left sat a glistening pond, reflecting the purple and orange hues of twilight. A rustic wooden dock nestled on its far bank, and on it stood a handsome fisherman. Stone looked her way and smiled, taking her breath away. Then he raised a finger to his lips and motioned her closer. Stone's fishing pole bowed as something pulled at the line. Melissa watched, mesmerized, while Stone deftly jerked back the rod and rapidly reeled in a huge fish. It wriggled on the line, but Stone quickly dipped a net into the water and snatched it up before snaring the bass off the hook with a gloved hand and ditching it into an ice-filled cooler. He flipped the lid shut and grinned. "Looks like supper."

"Looks like a big one," Melissa said, still amazed.

"Yeah, they grow big out here," Stone responded. "A whole lot of supply and not enough demand."

"I didn't mean to disturb you," Melissa said. "In fact, I didn't realize you lived over this way." Her eyes scanned the small split-log structure. "Is that your cabin?"

"Has been lately."

"Looks homey."

She gazed up at him and Stone fell into her eyes. "It is," he said with a struggle, speaking past his scratchy throat. Her hair was long and loose and her cheeks tinged pink with the cold. She was probably even prettier than he remembered. But somehow, in seeing her now, it seemed Stone had always known her face. As if it had been etched in his soul.

Her color deepened and her lips parted slightly. For a lunatic instant Stone had the instinct to kiss her. To take her in his arms and hold her close. "It's pretty out here," she said.

"Sure is," Stone replied, never taking his eyes off hers. "Especially at sunset."

"Yes."

An invisible cord stretched between them, momentarily tying each one to the other. Then Melissa lowered her eyes to his tackle box and the spell was broken. "Good fishing today?"

"Not as good as some," he answered honestly. "But good enough for eating. Say..." he said, a thought occurring. "There's plenty enough for two..."

"Oh no, I couldn't." But despite her words, it appeared she wanted to. She bit her bottom lip, as if reconsidering, then said unconvincingly, "I've got work to do."

Stone glanced at the descending sun. "You work late."

"Sometimes I have to."

"And what work is that, exactly?"

"I write music," she told him. "Compose melodies for background scores."

"Scores, as in for movies?"

She nodded modestly, but Stone couldn't help but be impressed. "Wow, Melissa. That's very cool. Any that I might have heard of?"

"Most are made-for-television movies and targeted at a female demographic, so maybe not." She laughed and he chuckled in return.

Stone set his rod against the dock railing. "Try me."

"*Love's Return?*"

Stone shook his head.

"*Same Time Tomorrow? The Man of My Dreams?*"

A smiled creased his lips. "You're right, I'm sorry. I don't know any of them."

"Then we won't even get started on the soap operas," she said with a teasing lilt.

Stone bellowed a laugh. "I'm afraid I'd be helpless there."

She met his eyes, then said lightly, "I finally met your grandfather."

"Ah, the captain…" he said with understanding. "He stopped by?"

"Yes, didn't he tell you?"

"No, not yet."

"Well, it was only this morning," Melissa continued. "He was full of stories about this property."

Stone eyed her thoughtfully. "I hope you won't take those legends too seriously. Nothing to them, really, but a bunch of bunk."

"What about Fiona and Lewis?"

"Oh, they were real, all right. So's their tragic tale as far as I can tell. But that was over a century ago."

"Captain Bill says I look like her," Melissa said, surprising him.

"Like who? Fiona?"

Melissa nodded uncertainly. "I know it sounds a little weird. Could just be my coloring, or something. Anyway…" Her brow rose with the question. "Just how would he know?"

"There's probably a picture around here somewhere," Stone said, struggling with the memory.

"Have you seen one?"

He *had* seen an old photograph. That's right. In the memory box. "Yeah, but it's been ages." He studied Melissa's face a moment, making a mental comparison. Both were certainly beautiful and had fair complexions, but in Stone's mind the likeness ended there. "Captain Bill probably just meant to flatter you," he said cordially.

"I didn't take Captain Bill to be the flattering kind," Melissa bantered.

"No, but *I* am. Is that what you're thinking?" He gazed at her deeply and Melissa flushed. "From what I saw, Fiona was very pretty," Stone said. "But she didn't hold a candle to you."

Stone cursed himself for flirting and pushing things too far. But seriously, how could he help it when a woman looking and smelling as pretty as Melissa stood this close? Her honeysuckle scent wafted toward him, all sexy and feminine. It made Stone want to be all male. *And all hers.* Stone imagined bringing his mouth down hard on the soft cushion of Melissa's lips and stifled a moan.

"I'm sorry that I troubled you," she said, backing away. "I mean, interrupted your fishing." Her cheeks were still pink and the tip of her nose burned bright red. Either she was feeling the nip in the air or Stone had desperately embarrassed her. She glanced down at his fishing rod, then over at his cabin. "I'm sure you have better things to do."

Normally, Stone didn't mind what other people thought of him. He had plenty of money and his lifestyle suited him for now. Besides, he had his eye on doing more someday. Something really big. "Melissa," he said, speaking hoarsely. "This isn't all I plan to do, you know."

Melissa feared she'd insulted Stone without meaning to. It seemed as if he thought she'd judged him, and found him lacking. But that wasn't the case at all. There was so much about him she didn't know, and more she wanted to learn. "I'm sorry, I didn't mean to imply… What I meant was, I imagine you stay really busy around here."

"Around here?" he echoed. Stone glanced around the clearing, then back at his cabin before meeting her eyes. "Yeah, but someday…" His words fell off and he appeared serious for a moment, as if he were weighing how much he wanted to tell her. Soft gusts of winds blew, fanning through her hair.

"Yes?" she pressed.

Stone surveyed her features and heaved a sigh.

"Never mind," he said resolutely. "It's not important."

Melissa worried that she'd been too intrusive. Stone probably lived this kind of life because solitude was what he craved. Not chatty conversation with a lonely woman. Melissa swallowed hard, grasping the reality. That's exactly what she was. Though she'd tried to convince herself she was happy with her work and her friends, Peter's leaving had left a searing hole in her heart. One she'd initially thought would be impossible to mend. Now she found herself questioning whether starting over was possible after all. Not with Stone himself, of course. But with someone equally kind and caring, a person who could take her for who she truly was. "Well, I suppose I'd better get back to the house, and my project," Melissa said, excusing herself. "I'd hoped to get a little more work done by the end of the day."

"Guess that beats playing well into the night." Stone beheld her kindly. "Not that I minded the serenade."

"I'm sorry?" Melissa said, not understanding.

"Last night," he told her. "I heard you playing. It had to have been well after midnight, maybe even closer to three a.m."

Melissa gasped with alarm. "That's impossible," she told him, certain she'd slept soundly the whole night through.

"No worries, your insomnia secret's safe with me." He shot her a wink and Melissa's heart fluttered, even as her head still reeled at his ridiculous allegation. She most clearly had not been playing the piano late at night, nor had she heard it being played, either. That's when it occurred to Melissa that Stone was likely teasing her again, simply trying to play into that silly legend.

"I get what this is," she said with a knowing smile. "You're telling ghost stories."

"Ghost stories?" Stone questioned with staged confusion. Boy, he was good. Completely poker-faced. Melissa wasn't about to let Stone's sense of humor get the better of her this time. There had been no piano playing last night, let alone by her.

"Can't fool me, Stone," she said good-naturedly. "But it was fun of you to try!"

Then she turned and sashayed back toward the house, leaving Stone standing there by his tackle box, appearing confounded.

Chapter Seven

Stone watched Melissa disappear through the trees, then he gathered up his gear. It was funny how she hadn't wanted to admit to the late-night playing. Then again, he supposed she'd been embarrassed that he'd heard her. She probably hadn't realized his cabin was so nearby and had believed herself to have total privacy. Well, she did for the most part. Stone would just have to stay out of her way and let her get her work done. She'd paid for a solitary getaway, so who was Stone to try to complicate that by extending inane invitations to dinner? While it had seemed to flow naturally during their discourse, Stone now felt embarrassed for even bringing it up. He'd put Melissa in a spot where she'd had to politely decline. What would make Stone think a woman like her would have an interest in the likes of him anyway? She was clearly accomplished and had a very impressive career. Unlike Stone, who'd found himself floundering like a wayward fish discarded at the edge of a bank. Stone didn't intend to do this forever, but he was still getting his bearings. The moment he felt centered, he planned to focus all his energy on developing the museum.

The idea had been in the back of his mind for some time now. But it was unformed, like a rough gemstone that needed sculpting and polishing. When Stone was only eight years old, his father, David, had given him a memory box. It was midsized and made of weathered wood. With its brass hinges and steel clasps, it looked almost like an old-time treasure chest. And what treasures it contained: all sorts of memorabilia from the ancestors in his family, stretching back through generations of kinfolk who had worked the seas, way back to his great-great-grandmother Mary's brother, Lewis Stone. Stone had been given the family surname as a first name, as no direct male heirs had survived to carry on the last name. Though Lewis Stone had never married, his sister, Mary, had. She'd produced two daughters, Adelaide and Amelia, and one infant son, Henry, who'd died shortly after birth. Adelaide had remained a spinster, but Amelia had married, producing three girls of her own. One of those girls was Jocelyn, Stone's grandmother on his father's side.

Jocelyn had been a red-haired, gray-eyed beauty with a natural affinity for men of the sea. She'd married Stone's grandfather, Captain William Thomas, and they'd made their home in Port Scarborough. Bill and Jocelyn raised two sons: Garrett, who'd died in his twenties in combat, and Stone's dad, David. Stone had been raised by his paternal grandfather after his parents' untimely death during a violent autumn hurricane. His maternal grandparents had lived several states away and had not been in good health. Together, his grandparents agreed that Stone would be better off staying in Virginia with Bill, who was a widower then, while taking regular trips to visit his mother's side of the family. Stone had been in his sophomore year of high school and had resented the move from the bustling naval base at Norfolk to this nearly nonexistent

community on the Virginia Eastern Shore. The moment
he'd graduated from high school Stone had taken off
for the Caribbean, determined not to look back. But
after ten years away, Stone *had* looked back, and he'd
felt called to come home. Especially after the accident,
he'd been compelled to get his life in order. Set his
mind on actually accomplishing something, rather than
simply existing from day to day.

That's where the memory box came into play.
Stone had held on to it for over two decades, leaving it
in his old bedroom at Bill's house during his time away.
When he'd moved into the cabin, Stone had brought it
with him, but he'd only recently begun to sense its
importance. There was so much history tied to this
community and the people who lived here, and their
stories were rich and worth telling. Stone was
convinced that if he could gather enough historic items
from other families in the area, he'd have the
beginnings of a truly fascinating maritime museum.
One that he could operate and own, so that the struggles
and successes of Port Scarborough's forebears might be
preserved for future generations. It was a worthy goal,
but it would take some doing to accomplish it. Not that
Stone doubted he was up to the task.

Stone left his fishing gear on the front porch and
carried the cooler into his cabin. Shadows haunted the
inside walls and stretched long across broad floorboards
as the woodstove emitted a warming glow. He'd add
another log to the fire and get started on supper. It was
bound to be delicious. Stone fought off a tinge of
melancholy as he found himself thinking he secretly
wished he'd be serving dinner for two. Melissa Carter
was an incredibly interesting woman: gifted and
intelligent, and just about as gorgeous as any woman

he'd seen. And when she looked into his eyes, it was almost as if she could see right through to his heart. Or perhaps it was more like she *wanted* to see him…desired the opportunity to get to know him better. Stone wondered if that part was true, or whether his imagination was simply getting the better of him. One thing he hadn't imagined was that piano playing. He'd heard it as clear as day, and Stone had a sneaking suspicion he'd be hearing it again. Maybe even later tonight.

Chapter Eight

Melissa slept fitfully, tossing and turning from side to side. It was like something was pulling her along…calling her through a fog. And then there was the music: hauntingly eerie, seeping up through the floorboards just beneath her bed and reverberating off the walls. Melissa flipped over again and the sheets twisted around her, wrapping her body in a tight cocoon. She was a ship torn from its moorings and cast adrift on a tumultuous sea. The room whirled around her at a dizzying tilt. She tried to kick her legs, but they were bound tightly, and her arms pinned beneath her felt numb. She was panting heavily now, struggling to catch her breath. Then she was running, racing toward the water shrouded in billowing fog. Off in the distance, she spied full sails ahead. The ship was steering in her direction. It was coming in to port! *My true love is coming home.*

Melissa's eyes popped open to meet the dark of her room. Faint hints of moonlight poured through the windows, painting translucent stripes along the floor. Across the room stood the open door, gaping inward and exposing the gloomy hallway that would lead her downstairs and then outdoors. Melissa sat up in a trance and peeled away the tight bedding. Her extremities tingled and her heart raced as the glorious tune played on. But this time it wasn't a piano she heard; it was the song of the wind, beckoning her with graceful fingers crooked toward the dock on the cove. Melissa set her feet on the floor, her gaze pinned to the window. She stood and floorboards creaked, moaning as she made her way across them, then slowly down the stairs. This house was sad and so was her heart. She'd waited an eternity. Longer than forever. But finally, her waiting was over.

Stone awoke with a start to the raucous assault of sound. Piano music pealed through the night, batted about on the wind. This piece wasn't serene and soothing like the one he'd heard before. It was brutal, almost angry: each violent strike of the keys pounding with more desperate force than the one before. An ominous feeling gripped him, squeezing so tight that Stone feared he couldn't breathe. He gasped for air and leapt from the bed. Something was terribly wrong.

The music continued at a fever pitch as Stone raced for the door. But when he yanked it open, Stone encountered nothing but whistling winds. Stone cautiously eased out onto the porch, listening again. Cool breezes blew as patchy dark clouds skittered across the moon. That's when Stone glimpsed something in the distance. Beyond the field and its pond stood a winding footpath. From this angle on the porch he could see around its bend to where the dock stretched out onto the water. Melissa was walking along it, barefoot and in only a nightshirt. Gusts of air combed through her hair, sending it flying behind her, as she strode forward with zombie-like steps. Panic seized Stone with the certainty: *she's not going to stop!*

Stone slammed shut the cabin door and raced down the stoop, tearing across the icy field. Briars scratched his feet and twigs and rocks poked up at him, but Stone ran on, zooming toward the dock. She had to be sleepwalking and not in her right mind, because she was nearly to the edge and about to step off into the water. It was over twelve feet deep at that end, deep enough to quickly submerge her, plus the waters were frigid. Stone raced down the footpath and onto the grassy stretch adjoining the water. Then he was up on the dock, uneven nail pops tearing at his soles as he went. His footfalls thrummed against the floating walkway, sending it wobbling beneath him. But if Melissa noticed, she didn't react. "Melissa!" Stone gave a desperate cry as she lifted one foot in the air just above the water. Then he lurched forward and grabbed her from behind.

Melissa shrieked at the force of arms wrapping around her, clamping her to a muscled chest. Then she was lifted off her feet and hoisted backward, away from a gleaming abyss. All at once Melissa was aware of the cold and the feel of a heartbeat thundering behind her. It pounded against her back in a frantic rhythm as Stone's voice huskily called, "Melissa!" Slowly he set her down and Melissa doubled forward, feeling as if she might retch. He steadied her with a hand on her shoulder. "Just take it easy," he said in a calming tone, his breathing labored. "Catch your breath."

Melissa gulped in air, not understanding. Why was she here? On the dock on the cove? Chill bumps raced up her bare legs and prickled her arms. The wind gave an angry howl and she shuddered again. "Come here," he said, "you're freezing."

She shakily turned toward him to find Stone standing on the dock wearing sweatpants and a plain white undershirt. Her head spun and Melissa's knees buckled. Stone took her in his arms, shoring her up against him in the windy night. "What happened?" she asked, gazing up at him with incredulity.

His head dipped toward hers, his eyes catching a glimmer of moonlight. "You must have been sleepwalking."

"Out here?" Melissa's voice rose in a panic and she shivered.

Stone tightened his embrace until the front of her body was plastered to his. "We should get you indoors."

Melissa nodded numbly, not sure how any of this had happened. She thought she recalled a dream, but it was vague now, quickly fading away like a rising plume of smoke above a candle's extinguished flame.

Stone viewed her with concern. "Do you think you can walk?"

She nodded again, but when she took a tentative step away from him, her legs gave way. Stone reached for her quickly, catching her behind the knees and snatching her up in his arms. He cradled her against his chest and looked down at her. Shadows outlined his rugged features. "Maybe this way is better."

Melissa met his eyes and deep in her soul something caught fire. It started with a tiny spark of longing, then blazed full-force like a secret, burning desire. Who was Stone Thomas and why did she feel she knew him? What's more, why did she find herself falling into him…into a heady downward spiral from which there might be no return? She spoke in a breathy whisper, not trusting anything about herself at the moment. Not the strength of her legs nor the logic of her hopelessly irrational heart. "Yes."

Stone smiled warmly and carried her toward the farmhouse with long, steady strides. Melissa glanced back at the water and the dark shimmering ripples of Homecoming Cove. The glassy surface appeared pockmarked by tiny darts falling from the sky. When she felt the prickles against her bare skin, Melissa realized it was raining.

Chapter Nine

Melissa handed Stone a mug of hot tea as he sat on the sofa. He'd started a fire for them in the hearth while Melissa had gone to change into dry clothing and turn on the kettle. When he'd bent down to stoke the hearth, Stone had noticed a streak of red on the hardwood. That's when he'd seen the small gash in his heel and realized he must have hit a nail pop on the dock. Stone's eyes trailed to the back door through which he'd entered, spying the bloody footprints. Great. Now he was making a mess. Stone lit the fire, then carefully ambled to the kitchen to grab some paper towels and a few items from the first-aid kit the owners kept under the sink. By the time Melissa returned downstairs, he'd already mopped up the floor and had situated himself back in the living room as if nothing were amiss.

Thunder boomed outdoors and lightning ripped through the sky above the cove, which was visible during periodic bright flashes through the large living room windows. Stone pulled his gaze from the dock to meet Melissa's eyes. "The tea is delicious, thanks."

Melissa settled into a seat that was catty-corner from his, wearing a sweatshirt and jeans and holding her own mug of tea. "I hope it's hot enough?"

"Perfect."

She studied Stone with a worried frown. "You're wet. I wish I had something that would fit you."

Stone chuckled to himself, thinking that was unlikely. The woman was nearly half his size. "I'll dry out here," he said, motioning to the fire. Logs crackled and hissed, emanating a warming glow.

Melissa seemed to notice for the first time the flat gauze pad and small length of Ace bandage he'd wrapped around his wound. "Your foot!" she cried, taken aback. "You're hurt." She met his eyes with concern. "Did that happen out—?"

"No big deal, really," he said with a shrug. "Just a little jab."

"Maybe I should take a look?" That was all Stone needed: Melissa playing Florence Nightingale. Stone hadn't had a woman look after him since…since he didn't know when. Stone had learned to look after himself. Most days, he did a pretty good job with it.

"All taken care of it," he assured her. "Should be as good as new by morning." Stone shot her a wry smile. "I'm up on my shots, you know."

"Well, I'm sorry. Sorry that happened on account of me."

A little nick was a small price to pay for Melissa's safety, and he said so. She smiled gratefully, then eyed him over the rim of her mug. "I appreciate your staying for tea. I don't think I could have gone right back to bed after what happened."

"I don't blame you," he said sympathetically. "That must have been quite a shock, waking up like that and finding yourself headed into the water."

"I'm just lucky you were there to save me." She ducked her head with a blush. "I mean, catch me before I walked off the dock completely."

"What could have made you go down there?"

"I don't know." She hesitated, glancing briefly toward the windows. "The whole thing is fuzzy now. Somehow I think it had something to do with what I was dreaming… And maybe it was about the music, too."

"Music?" Stone set down his mug and angled forward on his elbows. "You were playing again," he asked, "weren't you?"

"No!" She blinked, then seemed to collect herself. "I mean, I couldn't have been."

"But I heard you. That's what woke me."

Melissa stared at him, her expression blank. "It couldn't have been me, Stone."

"How do you know you weren't playing in your sleep? You went walking, didn't you?"

"Yes, but…" Her voice faltered. "Play the piano without knowing it? I seriously doubt I'm capable of that. I certainly couldn't play while I'm sleeping."

Stone settled back against the sofa and stroked his chin. Melissa appeared convinced of what she was saying, but then what other explanation was there for what he had heard? Not just once, but twice now, since Melissa's arrival. Sure, Stone had heard those silly ghost stories about the old piano playing itself, but he definitely didn't believe them. With an accomplished pianist in the house, there was a rational reason that old instrument had been making sound. That reason's name was Melissa. Naturally, that notion would freak her out. The phenomenon of Melissa playing in her sleep had apparently never happened before. Then again, Stone doubted very seriously she'd ever woken up walking off a dock and into Homecoming Cove, either. Stone decided the best course right now was to agree with what she said and try not to antagonize her. She'd already been through one upset this evening. No sense in forcing this other issue. "You're right," he answered in placating tones. "It's unlikely you could have done that. Perhaps I was having weird dreams, too."

"Do you?" Her blue eyes met his. "Sometimes have strange dreams of your own?"

Stone thought of his recurrent nightmares. "I suppose everyone does once in a while," he hedged, not wanting to discuss them.

"Yes, I suppose so."

Stone examined her face in the firelight, the soft curve of her cheeks and the full line of her mouth, and he felt a silent calling inside. It was a face he knew so well, yet not at all. What on earth could he be thinking about? "How about you?" he asked, redirecting. "Are you plagued by bad dreams?"

"Not usually. At least, I can't remember them." She sighed, then took a slow sip of tea. "Maybe it's this place. Or perhaps your grandpa's stories."

"Ah, Captain Bill." Stone smiled fondly. "He loves that story about Lewis and Fiona."

"But why, when it's so sad?"

"I guess it's a bit of family lore he likes passing on."

Lightning flashed outside, tearing up the night.

"*Your* family's lore?" Melissa asked with surprise.

"Well, sure. But going back generations." He stopped and studied her puzzled expression. "I guess he didn't tell you."

"Tell me what?"

"Lewis Stone was my great-great-grandmother's brother, an ancestor on my father's side. I was named after him."

Melissa paused a long while. "Really?" she finally said. "But this house…" She glanced around the living room, then out to the porch and back toward the kitchen. "It doesn't belong to your family any longer?"

"Never did," he told her firmly. "Fiona's father bought it for her, and as a gift to the engaged couple. This property was to be part of her dowry."

"But the wedding never occurred," Melissa said, reiterating what Captain Bill had told her.

"Unfortunately, no."

"Then, how did you and your grandfather come to be here?"

"It's a long story."

"I've got all night." She smiled encouragingly and Stone's heart pitter-pattered. For an instant, he had an inkling Melissa could convince him to say anything…spill all sorts of secrets.

"All right," he said, acquiescing. "Here's the abbreviated version. After Fiona's death, the deed was passed to someone else in her family, a distant cousin I think. It stayed in that family for years, but no one ever came to visit and nobody looked after the property. Basically, it fell into disrepair. Years later, a wealthy Bostonian was in the area, taking his daughter to view the wild ponies up in Chincoteague. They passed through Port Scarborough and this man—his name was Brandon—was taken with it. He decided to buy a vacation home on the Virginia Eastern Shore and started asking around about what was available."

"So he bought the House at Homecoming Cove," Melissa surmised.

"Bought it and completely renovated it, soup to nuts."

"When was this?"

"Sometime in the nineteen nineties. Only recently, his heirs decided to sell the place, so they made some additional improvements, but so far…"

"They're not having much luck," Melissa finished for him.

He nodded in agreement and genuine interest shone in her eyes.

"What about the garden?" she asked.

"Garden?"

"The old rose garden. It's the only piece of the property that looks like it isn't being taken care of."

"That's because the Brandons are intending to tear it down."

"What? How awful. But why?"

"They've talked about extending the patio and putting in a hot tub. I suppose they think it might help this place sell. They had some landscapers out here drawing up plans just last month, right before you booked your rental."

"Well, I think it's sad they'd let the rose garden go. It's such an important part of the landscape. I'm sure it contributed to Homecoming Cove's original beauty."

"Yes." Stone met her gaze and something sparked between them. He wondered if she was contemplating what he was: how gorgeous the garden would look in full bloom. He'd seen it that way years before, but since his recent employment at Homecoming Cove it had been left to lie fallow. He continued, addressing her original question.

"Anyway, my granddad was hired on to work the place when the Brandons first bought it. They lived mostly out of state and needed someone close at hand to keep it up on a regular basis. Captain Bill had just retired from running a small deep-sea fishing operation.

He had extra time on his hands, so he applied for the position here and he got it."

Melissa sat listening with rapt attention, waiting for Stone to finish his story.

"When I was a kid, I went to live with Captain Bill after my parents died."

Melissa's eyes brimmed with sadness. "Oh Stone, I'm so sorry. About your folks. I had no…"

"It's all right," he said, as much to reassure himself as her. "That was a long time ago." Stone set his lips in a hard line and turned toward the fire, watching the flickering blue and gold flames. When he turned back to her, he said, "In any case, when I moved up here, Captain Bill was already running the place. I helped him out when I could. Then, after high school, I moved away for a while, before eventually returning to Port Scarborough."

"There's no place like home," she said softly.

Emotion clogged his throat. "No, there's not," he answered. "And I guess this *is* home to me. It's not where I lived when I was little, but it's where I went to high school."

"And the place you returned to," she said astutely, "after your time away." She finished the last of her tea and set down her mug. "Where did you go?"

"Aruba."

She laughed with pleased surprise. "Wow!"

"And Antigua…Barbados…Saint Thomas…Saint John's…"

"How exotic." She appeared both delighted and fascinated, which left Stone with an inexplicable drive to both laugh out loud and hug her. It was almost like he'd seen her look that way—and had felt that urge— before. All at once she was upbeat and lively, and Stone could almost envision sweeping her up against him and carrying her across a dance floor.

"What were you doing there?"

"Crewing sailboats for the very rich," he said, grinning.

"What made you stop?"

Stone shrugged. "I decided it was time to come back here."

"Yes, well…" She studied him a long moment, then her cheeks colored brightly. "I'm awfully glad that you did."

"I'm glad too."

Silence stretched between them as embers popped and the fire waned. Stone was at war with himself, wanting to stay yet wanting to go. Things were growing a little too comfortable between them. It was cozy sitting here with Melissa as the rain fell. But soon sitting across from her wouldn't be enough. Stone would want to move nearer. He already ached to be close to her and take her in his arms the way he'd done when he'd carried her across the back lawn and into the house. If he held her now, Stone couldn't trust himself with what he might experience next. A burning desire to kiss her, then carry her upstairs? He didn't know what it was about Melissa that called him, but he felt pulled, like shells lost to the drag of the sea. When she gazed at him with those blue eyes, Melissa definitely had the power to pull him under. He needed to leave now while he still had his wits about him.

"Well," Stone said, getting to his feet. "It's awfully late. Do you think you can sleep now?"

"Probably like a rock." She stood as well and offered to take his mug. He handed it to her and they both paused. Melissa's gaze washed over him and

Stone was caught up in her spell. She was so beautiful standing there—extraordinary. It would take everything he had to turn and walk away. Already he was swimming in her sweet perfume, lost in her heady proximity. Needing to cup his hand to her cheek…run his fingers through her long, silky hair, golden and luscious in the firelight. If she came any nearer, he was doomed.

Her words came out in a whisper. "Thank you for everything. For coming to my rescue, for…" She was saying good-bye, yet her chin tilted toward his and she took a step closer, her lips barely parted, inviting. She peered up at him and met his gaze with a look that was surprisingly heated, decidedly predatory. There was no mistaking it. Melissa wanted him too. That was all the encouragement Stone needed to take her in his arms and bring his mouth down on hers with a hungry desire that surpassed all expectations.

Melissa gasped with delight and sighed into his kiss. Stone's empty mug slid from her grasp and landed somewhere on the sofa. He pressed his eager body to hers and ran his hands up her back, threading his fingers through her hair. She was glorious, beautiful, her gaze sparking with reciprocal passion. Stone groaned and kissed her again, savoring the taste of her, delighting in the sweetness of her body molded to his, as his blood pumped harder and his heart beat like a kettledrum gone out of control. It was more than a kiss; it was like coming home.

"Stone," she said breathlessly. He opened his eyes to find his cheeks nestled between her palms. She looked up at him, her face flushed with longing. "I think you'd better go."

"Yeah," he said, his pulse pounding. "I'd better go."

Thunder boomed and rain slapped the windowpanes, while the fire hissed and moaned.

Neither one moved.

"Melissa," Stone whispered, brushing his lips over hers. "You and me... It's like... I don't know."

"I know," she replied, meeting his kiss. "I feel it too."

Chapter Ten

Melissa drifted off to sleep as if floating on a puffy cloud. Though her nightmarish ordeal had left her exhausted, Stone's presence had steadied her. He'd been so thoughtful and genuine in his concern. He'd been open about his background, too. So many of the people Melissa met in her business tended to keep to themselves. She'd found some of the men particularly standoffish, guarded in a way she didn't expect. It was almost like once they reached thirty, the more successful guys became very circumspect: wary of women latching on to them. Peter, an executive producer at one of the studios where she worked, had first struck her as that way, and initially she'd found his aloofness appealing. In the end, she'd realized that had merely been a reflection of his true character. Keeping his professional distance was one thing, but after he and Melissa had finished their contract together and they'd begun dating, that quality had remained.

Now Melissa understood that Peter had kept himself apart because he'd believed himself superior to her. His family had come from a clearly recorded line of descendants dating all the way back to the *Mayflower. New England Bluebloods,* he used to call them. Blue, ha! Melissa had eventually realized Peter's true color was yellow. While he'd been happy enough to date her and have her on his arm at certain social functions, Peter never would have become involved with her seriously. Not a person of such *ordinary* heritage. And he'd certainly never intended to marry her.

Melissa could still recall the impact of her jaw dropping when he'd actually had the nerve to say those very things. Melissa came from a good family in upstate New York. She had two caring parents, both schoolteachers, and an older brother who was a minister in Florida. Her father taught high-school history classes and her mom was an elementary-school music teacher, with a special giftedness in piano. She'd imbued Melissa with the love of music from an early age and had glowed with pride when Melissa secured her first adult job in music production, after graduating from a prestigious music conservatory.

Melissa's grandparents on both sides had passed, and they'd come from good stock too. A true history buff, Melissa had appointed herself the family genealogist, and had been able to trace her family records back to England and Germany. Her ancestors might not have come over on the *Mayflower*, but they'd apparently been honest, hardworking people, many of them tradesmen. Peter had found this somehow distasteful, and his disapproval had left a lingering bitter taste on Melissa's tongue. She was so much better off without him.

Melissa rolled onto her side and settled the pillow under her head, thinking of Stone. While she was just starting to know him, he didn't seem to be the kind of guy who'd judge a girl by her family's past. Stone appeared to be a man of integrity. Melissa found herself

wanting to know all the reasons for Stone's return to
Port Scarborough, and more about what had motivated
him to leave in the first place. He'd surprised her by
mentioning his stint in the Caribbean, and saddened her
with the revelation about his folks. She supposed it was
good Stone still had his grandfather, and a place to
come back to.

There was no question that Melissa was better off
for Stone being here. Just think of what might have
become of her if he hadn't appeared on the dock at
precisely the right moment. If she'd plummeted into the
cold water, unconscious and unawares, might she have
drowned during the ensuing jolt of confusion? Melissa
shuddered under the covers, then let the memory of
Stone's warm kisses roll over her like calming ocean
waves. She'd been so caught up in his swell that
nothing else had seemed to matter. Not the memory of
her former boyfriend, nor her faraway life in New York
City. When she'd been in Stone's arms, it had been all
about the two of them, and what they could give to—
and take from—each other. A rich tenderness mixed
with passion, containing enough heat to rival the hottest
flame.

Melissa knew she shouldn't have given in. Her stay
here was only temporary, and Stone was indirectly in
her employ as the property's caretaker. Yet it was hard
to feel remorse about something that had been so
incredibly wonderful. From the time Stone had lifted
her into his arms and carried her toward the house,
she'd been helplessly lost in his magic: the soothing
timbre of his voice, the curve of his sexy smile, the way
the dancing firelight had played against his smoky gray
eyes. And his kisses had made her knees weak and her
insides melt like butter. She'd felt so connected to

Stone, it was impossible to believe he was a new acquaintance and that she hadn't known him forever. Perhaps she was foolish to feel that way, but it was hard to deny what she felt in her soul.

The following morning, Melissa arrived in the kitchen as the coffeemaker was producing its heavenly aroma. She'd risen early, feeling fully rested, happy, and eager to start her day. The sun shone brightly, bathing the floor tiles, cabinets, and center island with its cheerful light. After the darkness of yesterday's storm, it felt so good to be alive—and here at Homecoming Cove. Melissa thought of Stone and giggled giddily, hoping he'd drop by. Otherwise, she might have to take an afternoon walk to check on the fishing.

Heat seeped through her body as she recalled the pressure of his lips against hers, and his skillful tantalizing kisses. It had taken enormous fortitude for her to eventually push him out the door, although both she and he knew it was the right thing to do. Already, in a dizzying turn, things seemed to be moving pretty fast. Thank goodness they'd both had the good sense to put on the brakes. Stone had left her with a parting smile and a wink, saying, "I'll see ya later." Almost as an afterthought, he'd shot her a captain's salute before heading out the door.

Melissa had laughed heartily, so full of unbridled joy. She'd never expected to come to Virginia's Eastern Shore and become involved, but fate had surprised her. *And, maybe fate's not such a bad thing,* she thought with a saucy grin. The coffee finished brewing and she poured herself a cup, her gaze snagging on the sign above the window. *May those who come together here, never fall apart.*

Well, Melissa found herself thinking, *that's a pretty tall order for a music composer from New York and a Caribbean sailor from Port Scarborough, but I wouldn't mind spending a little more time with Stone while I'm here.* A loud banging suddenly interrupted her thoughts and Melissa stared through the kitchen window. It was Captain Bill! He was hammering away with furor at something down on the dock. She decided to take her coffee outside and join him.

Chapter Eleven

Melissa slid a thick cable-knit sweater over the long-sleeve T-shirt and sweatpants she'd slept in, then headed outdoors. Steam hovered above the coffee mug as its rising heat met the chilly morning air. The sun was halfway up over the water, sending shimmering glimmers of light across the cove and bouncing up into the trees that ringed it with rustling fall foliage. Captain Bill heard her approaching the dock and looked up. He clenched an unlit pipe in his teeth and held a battered old hammer. He was stooped down on one knee in an old field coat and wore gloves that had his fingertips exposed at the ends. On his head, a gray sea captain's tam sat slightly off kilter. "Morning!" he called loudly, taking her in.

"Good morning!" Melissa smiled and strode toward him. "It's a beautiful one."

"Calm after the storm, I suppose." Captain Bill set down the hammer and stood, dusting his hands on his faded jeans. "Sorry about the banging. Did I wake ya?"

"Not at all," she replied. Then she glanced down at the dock to see what he'd been doing.

"Nail pops," he explained without her having to ask. "Noticed 'em when I was out here the other day.

Figured they needed fixing. Never know when someone might come along here barefoot and hurt themselves."

"Yes," Melissa said, thinking of her episode last night and Stone's injury. "Isn't Stone the one who normally looks after—?"

"This kind of thing? Not really." Bill withdrew the pipe from his teeth and shoved it in his pocket. "I tend to the house and fixtures. Boy looks after the lawn."

"I see." Melissa glanced around curiously, foolishly hoping for a sign of him. "Is he here this morning, too?"

Bill shook his head. "Mac sent him up yonder to Deltaville to pick up some parts."

"Mac?" Melissa questioned.

"Stone's boss over at Bait, Tackle, and Motor. Place run by Jim McCoy."

"Oh!" Melissa said with unmasked surprise. She'd had no idea Stone had another job.

"Stone does hull patching for him. Tinkers with engines and makes 'em better, too. My grandson's got a lot of talents, you know."

He studied Melissa a long beat, as if surmising that she did. "You couldn't possibly have thought Stone had enough to do around here to keep him busy?"

Melissa's cheeks warmed. "No, I…"

"Least he didn't *used to* have enough around here to keep him occupied." A spark of understanding lit in Bill's eyes and Melissa felt her color deepen. "Times change, I suppose."

Melissa took a hurried sip of her coffee, which had gone lukewarm. "Captain Bill," she said, braving the topic. "I was wondering if you could tell me a little more about Lewis and Fiona."

Bill's blue eyes twinkled. "Liked that story, did ya?"

Melissa wasn't sure *liked* was the right word. "I was very intrigued by it."

"I already told you most of what I know."

Ever since Stone had mentioned being descended from Lewis, Melissa had found herself curious about Fiona's family. "I understand that Stone has a faraway connection to Lewis. I was wondering about Fiona and the cousins she had who took over this place?"

Bill eyed her astutely. Then he pulled out his pipe and stoked and lit it. "I didn't tell you any of that," he said between curly white puffs. "Ya must have been talking to Stone."

Melissa swallowed past her embarrassment. She didn't know why she should hesitate in admitting she and Stone had had a casual conversation. It wasn't like Captain Bill could possibly have guessed what had transpired between Melissa and Stone afterward. "Well, yes. Yes, in fact, that's right. When I saw Stone, he mentioned it."

Captain Bill viewed her suspiciously, then clucked his tongue. "Well, then. I guess you know all there is to know."

"Stone told me about his side of the family," Melissa pressed, "and about how it's traced back to Lewis, but Fiona—?"

"No living relatives to speak of," Captain Bill cut in. "There were some distant cousins who inherited this place, but when they passed, that was the end of the line."

"How do you know?"

"Property went through probate," he answered. "Before those new folks, the Brandons, could buy it, the courts had to be sure no living heirs were around to claim it. Attorneys conducted searches, notices were put in the papers. Nothing ever came of it."

"Where did the cousins live? The ones who first inherited the place?"

"Nevada."

Melissa's brow rose in surprise. "That's awfully far away."

"It is at that," Bill agreed. "Fiona's family moved there a long time back. Shortly after Nevada was settled as a state, her father joined the Union Army. He was only a kid then, about fifteen. He stayed up north during Reconstruction and worked as an apprentice for a shipbuilder. He accompanied his boss on a business trip to Virginia, where he met and fell in love with a Southern belle."

"Fiona's mother?" Melissa guessed.

Bill nodded. "She was from right around here. Her father ran a lumberyard. Supplied timber for housing construction and local boatbuilding. When Fiona's parents married, her dad moved to Port Scarborough and took over his father-in-law's business. He was a grown man then, twenty-five or twenty-six. Fiona was born the following year."

"What about brothers and sisters? Did Fiona—?"

"Not a one," Bill responded. "Her poor mother, Marjorie, died in childbirth, and her heartbroken father never remarried." He drew in on his pipe, then exhaled a long ribbon of smoke. "So, you see, after the demise of Fiona and those Nevada cousins, that really was the end of the line."

"I see." Melissa's heart sank. Well, what had she anticipated? That a descendant of Fiona's was still out there somewhere? It was a reasonable expectation, but Melissa now understood it had been a faulty one.

"That's too bad," she told Bill. "It's a shame the property fell out of Fiona's family."

"The family she had didn't take care of it," Bill answered brusquely. "Better off with the Brandons. Least they hired me." He flashed her a grin and Melissa noticed his teeth were uneven and brownish, probably from years of pipe smoking.

"Everything here certainly seems in good order now," Melissa agreed, opting not to mention the garden, as Stone had explained its condition anyhow.

"I thank ya," he said with pride. "Stone and I work at it."

"You do a fine job," Melissa stated pleasantly.

She glanced down at the hammer. "Well, I don't want to keep you from your work…"

"No trouble." His expression warmed. "It's been nice chatting."

As she started to walk away, he called after her. "How's that piano working out?"

Melissa slowly turned on her heels. "Piano? Why, it's great, thanks. Plays like a charm!"

"That's good to know. I was worried it might have gone rusty…gotten out of tune or something." He smiled at her. "That's probably the only type of equipment neither Stone nor I knows how to fix."

"It's a really great instrument," she said. "A true work of art. I'm glad that it's here."

"Always has been," he told her. "One of the original things, ya know."

"It was Fiona's," Melissa said, making the natural assumption.

"*She* knew what to do with it. That part's pretty much guaranteed."

"Fiona enjoyed playing?" Melissa ventured.

"More than enjoyed. She was exceptional at it. World-class concert pianist."

"Really?" Melissa asked, amazed.

"Traveled up and down the East Coast to all the big cities: Washington, Philadelphia, Boston, New York... Also played in Europe, I hear."

Melissa was impressed. "That's quite an accomplishment for a woman of her time."

Bill nodded. "Even made records too. Those old ten-inch vinyls, the sort they played on Victrolas."

Melissa was captivated by this revelation. She'd had no clue that Fiona had been such a talented and liberated woman. No wonder Lewis had lost his heart to her. "How fascinating. Do any of those records remain?"

"None that I've seen," he answered. He glanced toward the farmhouse and the pitch of its roof. "But you never know what's in the attic. There are a few boxes up there from way back that the Brandons have left untouched."

"You've never been tempted to look?"

He cracked an uneven grin. "Lady, they don't pay me enough for that."

Even in the warming sun, Melissa felt a sense of dread. "What's wrong with the attic?"

"Nothing at all. 'Cept nobody ever goes up there."

"Right."

"Don't want you going in, neither," he said with sudden urgency. "Can't attest to the safety of its structure. Things could come loose. Ya might get hurt."

Chapter Twelve

Even after Melissa had showered and dressed for the day, she could hear Captain Bill hammering away on the dock outside. She supposed she was glad he was making it safer. Melissa still felt terrible about Stone hurting his foot when he'd gone racing after her the night before. She hoped Stone was right and that his cut would heal quickly. Melissa was disappointed that he was away for the day, but understood he had work to do just as she did. It wasn't like one little kiss was going to change everything, and make the two of them forget about being responsible people. *Okay, so it was more than one little kiss. It was several. Deep...hot...spine-tingling, mouthwatering kisses.* Melissa felt steam rise off her skin and knew it wasn't the aftereffects of the shower. In only one evening, Stone had completely undone her. None of the other men who'd kissed Melissa had made her feel that way.

When Stone had taken her in his arms, he'd been easily in charge, in a skillful, commanding manner. It was as if all his force and focus were on her, and his unrestrained passion had made her weak with desire. She'd never had such an earth-shattering response to a man before. If Stone could make Melissa's heart race and her knees tremble just from his kisses, she could only imagine what it might be like to be made love to by such a man. A real man. Self-assured. Sexy. Strong. She'd already learned so many things about him.

Stone was a person who held on to his heritage, but he didn't let it hold him back. In fact, he seemed propelled forward by some masked ambition. He'd hinted at it earlier by the pond, then had seemed nearly prepared to confess something last night. Melissa couldn't help but wonder what Stone had in mind, or what sort of future he saw for himself. For Stone, it seemed the future was wide open. He had an easy confidence about him that most other men didn't possess. Many of the guys Melissa knew were ambitious and driven, yes. Most were also very successful. But those attributes often came at the price of a very sharp edge, which included a propensity for working long hours and at a frenetic pace. Melissa couldn't imagine any of those guys, much less Peter London, crewing a sailboat shirtless in the Caribbean. Stone Thomas was another matter, and the thought of the man half naked on a boat was enough to make Melissa want to jump back in the shower—and run it cold.

She shook off the thought with a giggle, feeling like a silly teenager with a crush. And to think: after Peter, she'd questioned her ability to become interested in another man. Her experience with Stone had totally turned things around. Her attraction to him felt brand new, yet somehow familiar. Inexplicably magical. Melissa bit her lip, recalling their sweet fireside exchange.

Was it possible that, in that brief moment, Stone had caught a glimpse of Melissa's soul—and she of his? What else could explain their instant connection, that feeling of *knowing* they appeared to have about each other? Melissa had read about soulmates and had even worked on projects portraying them. Some couples believed themselves to be fated. And even if they didn't see it at once, the audience could always tell immediately. Melissa had considered those stories highly sentimental and a tad over the top in their romanticism. She'd never believed that sort of thing *really* happened to people...until now. Melissa paused and gazed out her bedroom window at the dock, where Captain Bill still worked doggedly.

Perhaps she was being too dramatic. What if her connection to Stone was all in her head? Or worse, what if her reckless interest in Stone was pathetically one-sided? Melissa suddenly felt ashamed for making so much out of an isolated event. For all she knew Stone regretted their becoming physical. The next time she saw him, he might even say so and suggest that they forget it ever happened. Melissa's spirit sagged when she realized she'd probably overreacted to what was likely a one-time thing. A physical attraction that she and Stone had both given in to due to the lateness of the hour, the romantic music of the rain, and the waning firelight.

Melissa could fret all morning over missteps and possibilities, and wind up no more enlightened than she currently was. It would be far better for her to put some of that angst and energy to use by applying it to music composition. At least her music was something she was starting to bring under control. Melissa had recently learned she had much less skill at influencing men. Not that this mattered in the least. She hadn't come to Homecoming Cove to win over Stone Thomas, his grandfather, or anybody else. She'd come to complete her project, and that's just what she intended to do.

A little while later, Melissa sat at the piano making some new notes on her music pad. Though it was early, she'd fixed herself a light lunch of a sandwich and some chips and had carried it into the parlor along with a tall glass of water. She'd set them both on the low table perched beside a chair next to the piano. When she was in for a long stretch of writing, Melissa liked to set herself up to allow for minimal interruptions. She knew she'd eventually get hungry, but didn't want to stop in the middle of a riff and threaten derailing her creative energy. She was just trying out a new refrain when she heard a truck door slam shut and tires noisily crunch along the gravel drive. Captain Bill was finally leaving after having put in a full morning's work. Melissa understood that Bill, unlike Stone, didn't have a second job. He needed a place like this to keep him busy.

Melissa wondered if Bill got lonely living in such a remote location, but she supposed he had friends in Port Scarborough and got to see Stone often enough as well. Stone was another matter. While he was bound to have friends around too, this seemed like a really solitary life to lead for someone Stone's age. Melissa's mind drifted back to Stone's words when she'd caught him fishing. *This isn't all I plan to do, you know.* She had a sneaking suspicion that whatever his goals were, they had somehow brought him back here. Why else would a man like Stone return to Port Scarborough? Naturally, his grandfather was getting older and he probably wanted to help care for him. But Melissa had an inkling that wasn't all there was to it.

Her thoughts were startled by an abrupt crashing sound upstairs. Melissa sat stock-still, staring at the pad she'd propped up on the piano rack. Could that have come from her bedroom? There was no one else in the house. Melissa's heart pounded and her palms felt clammy. This was silly. There was a logical explanation for this somewhere, just as there'd been for that dancing curtain!

Something crashed down again and this time it was followed by a heavy thud, like a huge object had fallen. Melissa's pulse raced and perspiration swept her brow. *Stay calm*, she told herself, *I'm sure it's nothing.* Slowly, Melissa scraped back the piano bench and got to her feet. She listened intently, but heard nothing more. October winds blasted against the windowpanes, sending a loose one rattling in its frame. Melissa's gaze panned to the dock outdoors and then to the barn…and its neighboring garden. To her astonishment the garden gate creaked open. Melissa's heart hammered harder, as the gate gently swung open all the way, then began to slowly swing back and forth. Melissa exhaled sharply. *Of course, it's only the wind.* But then, what had she heard upstairs?

Melissa made her way to the stairs with trembling knees. She was foolish to feel afraid. All old houses made noises, and it was gusty outdoors. And what a beautiful day it was! Beautiful, bright, and sunny, completely in contrast to the drenching night before. If she'd heard creaks and bumps then, in the midst of that thunderstorm, she might have been reasonably spooked. Then again, if she'd heard them last night, she would have had Stone with her. Now Melissa was completely alone and more than thirty miles from the nearest town.

Which meant it was illogical to think another person was in the house. Melissa shuddered when she realized it wasn't a person she was worried about. Maybe she shouldn't have pestered Captain Bill about so many things from the past, like Fiona and Lewis and their tragic fate. It wasn't like either could still be around here, stealthily haunting the premises. Melissa was starting to freak herself out.

She swallowed hard and laid her hand on the banister, trying to think rationally. This was obviously some natural occurrence and she'd have a funny story to tell Stone the next time she saw him. A story that highlighted just how overwrought a big-city woman could become when left in the country for more than a couple days. Ha-ha. Truly hilarious. Stone would likely smile and say something reassuring. She couldn't wait to see him again.

Melissa took the flight of stairs and hesitated on the landing midway up, wondering if she should continue. Then she decided that if she didn't investigate things fully, she'd never have the peace of mind to get back to work. So she steeled herself and pushed ahead, trudging up the remaining steps, each riser seeming insurmountable as her legs felt trapped in quicksand. Finally at the top, she stopped and peered into the master bedroom, but everything seemed in order. She checked the other two bedrooms too, finding each in pristine condition. Melissa returned to the upstairs hall, then her gaze snagged on the door at the far end of the narrow expanse that stood catty-corner to the door to the master bedroom.

It was the door to the walk-up attic.

Chapter Thirteen

The moment Melissa reached the top of the attic stairs she was assaulted by a bright light and two dark creatures dive-bombing in her direction. Melissa shrieked and her arms jerked up to shield her face. She heard the flapping of wings and peered between her forearms, which she held high, one positioned in front of the other in a defensive block. Two fluttering black bats swooped through the dusty air, then zoomed in a pair through a gaping hole at the far end of the room. It was then that Melissa understood one of the attic vent coverings had caved in, exposing the shadowy attic to outdoor sunlight.

Relief flooded her veins. Naturally, the horrendous sounds had come from here. The fallen vent covering rested at an odd angle between the floor and a stack of boxes. It must have come loose and hit the boxes, then banged against the wall on its way down. That would have caused quite a ruckus in this cavernous space, and the sounds would have echoed—all the way through house. Melissa moved closer to study the rectangular vent covering. Hefting it into her hands, she found it surprisingly heavy. She examined its front and back, finding the paint on its outside slats chipped and its perimeter badly rotting. No wonder it had become dislodged in the strong winds. She'd need to call Captain Bill about this in the morning. She'd hate to trouble him again today, after he'd already put in so much work on the dock.

Melissa lowered the vent covering to the floor and leaned it against the attic wall beneath the opening at the pitch of the roof. Winds whistled through it and something fluttered in the corner of the room, catching her eye. Just beyond the stack of boxes that had broken the vent covering's fall sat an oddly shaped triangular object draped in a tarp. Melissa couldn't resist the urge to take a peek. She'd come up to the attic for a legitimate reason, after all. It's not like she'd arrived to snoop on purpose. Feeling a flush of excitement, Melissa reached for the tarp and carefully lifted it away from the object it concealed.

Sunlight gleamed against it, and Melissa fell back in awe. It was the most exquisite antique record player: the crank-up kind. One of the original Victrolas Captain Bill had been talking about. A perfectly preserved vinyl record sat on its turntable, as if it had been awaiting her discovery. Melissa admired the amazing relic, wondering how long it had been stored away. Then her eyes fell on the record label and she spied a woman's name. "Fiona," she whispered aloud.

A floorboard creaked behind her and Melissa yelped at the top of her lungs, spinning toward the door, her heart pounding. Stone stood at the top of the stairs wearing a puzzled look. "Melissa?" His gaze darted to the hole in the eave, then back to her. "What happened? Are you all right?" His eyes urgently traced the path from the vent's original position to where it now stood on the floor, leaning against the attic wall.

Melissa nodded, her hands trembling. "Two bats darted at me when I came up the stairs. I'd heard a loud noise in the attic, and when I came to investigate I found that," she said, indicating the vent covering.

Worry marred Stone's features. "You weren't hit when it came down?"

"No. I was downstairs."

Stone sighed audibly. "Thank goodness for that." He went and examined the vent covering as Melissa had done. "Looks like this needs replacing. I'll bring a new one by tomorrow."

Melissa was still in shock over his sudden appearance, not that she wasn't grateful he was here. "How…how did you get in?"

"Came through the screened porch. The back door wasn't locked. When I heard you scream, I worried it was an emergency."

"I thought you were in Deltaville?" she said, still dazed.

Stone grinned like he enjoyed the thought that she'd been keeping tabs on him.

"Was, but I made it a quick trip. Had some important business to take care of here." He met her eyes and Melissa's pulse quickened. "I wanted to check on you. Make sure you were okay after last night."

"That was really nice of you, Stone."

"I considered it a priority."

Heat rose in her cheeks. Melissa didn't think she'd ever been anyone's "priority" before, and it felt kind of nice. "Thank you."

Stone suddenly noticed what she was standing beside and gave a shrill whistle. "Man oh man, is that what I think it is?"

"It gets even better than that." His eyebrows rose and she answered him with a smile. "Guess whose name is on the record?" It didn't take him long to scan the label and read *Fiona Henderson, Philadelphia Concert Series.*

"It says 'series,'" Stone replied, "but it looks like that record only holds one piece."

"The series must have been recorded on separate discs and sold together as a set." Her eyes scanned the shadowy space near the base of the Victrola. "Like that one!" she exclaimed, her gaze landing on a labeled box containing the phonograph album.

Stone's grin lit up the dark corners of the room. "What do you say we bring them both downstairs?"

"I say we should."

"I'll carry the machine if you bring the records." His voice dropped huskily. "Then maybe we can open a bottle of wine to celebrate?"

"Celebrate?"

"It's a rare find, wouldn't you say? One of a kind." Smoldering gray eyes met hers and for a beat it sounded more like Stone was talking about her than the record player. Butterflies flitted about in her stomach, and her temperature rose.

"You open, I'll pour," she said shyly.

Stone gave a hearty laugh. "Agreed!" He rolled up his sleeves and appraised the Victrola. "First, let me take care of this."

Chapter Fourteen

Stone carried the Victrola into the living room and used a soft, clean cloth to gingerly wipe it down, removing every speck of dust. While the tarp had kept it protected, the old record player had obviously been sitting up in the attic for years. He used a separate rag to wipe off the ancient record, using great care not to track any grit across the surface. Stone was amazed by how solid the ten-inch disc felt, as well as by its girth. Its grooves appeared miles deep compared to the more modern-age vinyl records he'd seen. "Things back then were certainly built to last," he remarked to Melissa when she entered the room carrying a chilled bottle of wine, a corkscrew, and two glasses.

Stone placed the record back on the turntable and Melissa handed him the corkscrew and the bottle. "Will you do the honors?"

"My pleasure," he said jovially. Melissa couldn't believe how easy it was to be with him. It was impossible to think they'd only known each other for a couple of days and hadn't been acquainted for years. Stone tugged the cork from the bottle, then asked, "Want to carry our wine onto the porch? It's a nice evening out, not nearly as cold as it has been." As if sensing her question, he added, "We can leave the door ajar so we can hear the music from there."

"That sounds lovely." And it truly did. Melissa couldn't imagine anything more fantastic than sipping wine with a handsome man in a beautiful place, while listening to fabulous concert piano music. "Do you think the records will still play?"

"Let's crank up the Victrola and give her a whirl!"

Melissa filled their glasses while Stone set the machine in motion. Sound crackled out of the broad horn and Melissa resisted the urge to cover her ears. The next second, she was glad she had. The music began gently with a light tinkling of keys, and it was spellbinding.

"Amazing," she said catching her breath. "It sounds just—"

"Beautiful. Isn't it?" Stone lifted his glass and motioned toward the porch. "Shall we?"

Melissa couldn't have planned a more perfect evening. Rather than feeling pressed into conversation, both seemed content to absorb the view and appreciate the elegant music. They took turns changing the records, which only played for about three minutes each, and were increasingly amazed by Fiona's talent. "Fiona was incredibly gifted," Melissa said as the sun sank low on the horizon.

"So are you."

"Not quite concert material." Melissa laughed lightly. "I'd say my job is much more mundane that that."

"Who knows?" Stone said. "Maybe if Fiona had lived today, she'd be doing just what you are now."

"Hmm, maybe. But I doubt it. Her life was much more glamorous. Think of all the places she saw!"

"I doubt her life was that exciting. She probably traveled with a chaperone."

"I wouldn't have minded that!" Melissa said brightly. "Besides, maybe Fiona's chaperone had a sense of humor. Or..." she added impishly, "was a very sound sleeper."

Stone rumbled a laugh at this. "I think the legend of Fiona might be growing larger in your mind than she actually was."

"Perhaps," Melissa said. "But you've got to admit her story captures the imagination."

"Hers and Lewis's, you mean."

"Yes."

Stone studied the water and took a slow sip of wine. Suddenly, he turned back toward the house. "Hey, listen. Do you hear that?"

"What?" Melissa asked. "This new number? Yes, it's wonder—"

"That's not it." Stone shook his head with conviction. "It's the one."

"Which one?"

"The one I heard the other night. The first night you were here."

Melissa set down her wine. "That's impossible, Stone. We've only just now found the album."

"But I remember..." He set down his wine as well, and listened intently. "Yes, yes. I'm sure of it. The music I heard was whimsical, almost like a child's lullaby. If it wasn't this tune exactly, it sounded awfully close."

Melissa considered this a long while, then finally said, "No, no. I don't think you could have heard anything like that from me. I mean, there might be some common chords in one of the pieces I'm writing, but on the whole it's very different."

"If you say so." Stone heaved a breath and leaned back in his chair. "The truth is I'm not much of a musician. I probably wouldn't know a 'Yankee Doodle' from a 'Oh My Darling, Clementine.'"

Melissa gave a surprised laugh. "Most people wouldn't these days!"

"Oh, sorry," he said a bit sheepishly. "That's what I get for hanging around the geriatric citizens crowd. Pick up old-timers' expressions."

Melissa ribbed Stone back. "Ones even older than Captain Bill. He couldn't possibly remember those songs."

"Maybe his daddy shared them with him?" Stone ventured and Melissa laughed. Stone laid a hand on his heart and learned toward her with a serious look. "Promise you won't tell a soul," he whispered. "It will be the death of my social life in this town if word gets out I talk like an old fogy."

"No worries, your secret's safe with me." Melissa shot him a playful smile. "Not that there seem to be a lot of folks around here to tell, anyway."

"You just say that because you haven't been to Port Scarborough yet."

"A big metropolis, is it?"

"Bustling."

Melissa laughed again, feeling content and lighthearted. In the silence that followed, she and Stone realized the record had ended, and the needle was stuck in its final groove. "Shall we play them again?" she asked him. She was having so much fun with Stone, she couldn't bear for him to go.

"Are you inviting me to dinner?" he asked, appearing interested.

"You like spaghetti?"

Gray eyes twinkled. "It's my favorite."

Chapter Fifteen

Stone couldn't believe what a great time he was having. Everything had seemed to morph from just regular to fantastic upon meeting Melissa. Though he was deeply sorry she'd had that troublesome dream that led her on that dangerous walk, Stone would be forever grateful he'd gotten to her in time—thanks, in part, to the piano music that Stone was now starting to believe was something he'd *dreamed.* It was odd that the first tune he'd heard had sounded so much like the piece on Fiona's record. Then again, Stone wouldn't exactly consider himself an expert in music appreciation. Although, one thing was for sure: he certainly appreciated Melissa's gift.

"Do you think you could play for me sometime?" he asked as he refilled their wineglasses. They had moved on to red to go with the pasta, and now sat at the huge dining table beside a roaring fire. Once the sun had gone down, the temperature had dipped and Stone had offered to build a fire in the dining room while Melissa worked on dinner.

"I'd be happy to…" She shared a soft smile. "Sometime."

It felt very romantic, sitting here with candles burning on the table and a fire blazing in the hearth beside them. "That would be nice." Stone took another bite of food, savoring the tangy sauce made with garden vegetables. "This spaghetti's excellent," he said. "World's best."

"It's nice to have someone here to appreciate it."

"I appreciate everything about you, Melissa." Her cheeks colored sweetly. "Including the fact that you've taken in a rogue like me."

"I wouldn't exactly call you a rogue," she protested. But even as she said it, she was smiling. "Unless there's more to the Stone Thomas story you're not telling me."

"I think I filled you in pretty well." He took a sip of wine, then eyed her thoughtfully. "What about your story?"

"I don't know that there's much to tell."

"I doubt that," he said seriously. "A woman like you must have a fascinating past."

A sheen came to her eyes and Stone feared he'd made a misstep. He leaned forward and laid a hand on her arm. "I'm sorry, Melissa. I didn't mean to intrude."

Stone felt like a heel. What sacred ground had he trespassed on?

"I'm proud of who I am, you know." As she spoke, her chin trembled. "Of my parents and their parents before them. All good people."

"Of course you are. If your family's anything like you, they're bound to be wonderful."

"Tell that to Peter," she said flatly.

Uh-oh. Stone felt as if he'd moved from sacred ground onto an active minefield. "And Peter would be...?"

"An old boyfriend. *Ex*-boyfriend. Peter London. He could trace his bloodline back to the *Mayflower*. My heritage didn't measure up." She appeared downcast, as if recalling something very unpleasant.

"Sounds like good riddance to me." That was putting it mildly as far as Stone was concerned. This Peter London sounded like a raging jerk.

Melissa hesitated a moment, then spoke defiantly. "You know something? You're right."

She raised her glass in the air and Stone lifted his glass toward hers.

"What shall we drink to?" he asked.

"Not to old boyfriends, that's for sure." Stone was sorry to detect a sour note in her voice. He wanted things to go back to how they'd been on the porch, when Melissa had appeared congenial and happy.

Stone held her gaze and attempted to brighten her spirits.

"Well, then…" he began hopefully. "How about if we drink to new ones?"

Melissa flushed so violently, Stone feared she might burst into flames. "Stone! We've only just met!"

"I'm sorry," he said, worriedly. "I've embarrassed you."

She blinked incredulously. "I can't imagine why you would…? What I mean is… Did I say something to make you think that?"

Stone swallowed hard, feeling hot under the collar. And at his temples. Just about everywhere. A trickle of sweat dribbled down his back beneath his sweater.

"No!" Stone raced to supply a reasonable explanation that would set things back on track. His plan had backfired completely. Maybe if he made light of it and pretended to be joking, she would cut him some slack. "Melissa," he said quietly. "I was only teasing you."

That was a big fat lie and Stone knew it. He hadn't been teasing; he'd been testing. Stone didn't care about time frames. He liked Melissa and he enjoyed being with her, maybe even more than he'd enjoyed being with any other woman, and he'd recklessly hoped she liked him just as much. Plus, he'd wanted to get that blasted Peter London completely out of Melissa's mind. From the look on her face, Stone's entire strategy had been a major fail.

"Teasing?" Melissa's expression clouded over. "I see."

"I'm sorry," Stone said lamely. "It was a bad joke."

Melissa took a gulp of water, bright color staining her cheeks. "No… I think you're onto something." Melissa's eyes looked watery, as if she was on the verge of tears. She pursed her lips together, then she said coolly, "Let's do that, why don't we? Let's drink to new boyfriends." She smiled thinly and glanced around. "Wherever they may be!"

Melissa raised her glass and Stone clinked it weakly, fighting a sinking sensation in his gut. While the meal had been fine, Stone probably shouldn't be expecting any after-dinner kissing for dessert. In fact, Melissa seemed ready to get rid of him—posthaste.

Stone had really blown it this time. He'd pushed too hard and Melissa had shoved back. Well, maybe he'd deserved it. Who was he to go making presumptions, believing Melissa might be falling for him just as quickly as he was for her? Melissa clearly wasn't over her ex, and apparently wasn't interested in becoming seriously involved with anyone else, most especially Stone.

Melissa stood abruptly and snatched his plate out from under him. "If you're all done," she said, her lips quivering, "I'll just take this away." Then she cleared the dish, which still held half of his food. Stone sat there stunned while she strode toward the kitchen, her face bright red.

"Thanks for the dinner!" he called hoarsely after her. "It was delicious!"

It was all Melissa could do to keep herself together while she and Stone cleared the rest of the table. She'd told Stone to go on and that she'd take care of it, but for some reason he'd insisted on staying to help her. What did he want? To stick around and witness the outcome of his humiliation? It must have been extremely obvious to Stone how much she liked him. So much so that he'd gone so far as to mock her with the boyfriend bit. Melissa was painfully embarrassed to have been so transparent.

First, she'd spilled her guts about her family and then Peter…only to have Stone practically laugh in her face by calling her on her rampant crush. Melissa had wanted to sink into the floor that very moment. How could she have believed—even for a second—that Stone's interest in her was for real? So yeah, maybe he'd wanted a drink, and a meal, and a laugh… He'd sure gotten one, hadn't he? And the laugh was on her.

Stone stood on the kitchen threshold looking like a scolded puppy. "Melissa, if I said something to upset you, I honestly didn't mean it. It was just a…" He struggled with the word. "…joke between friends."

Ha-ha, very funny. A joke at her expense. It reminded her of all the times Peter had made fun of her, and when he'd attempted to belittle her feelings. She was *a silly, overemotional woman, one who became too quickly attached, and who expected too much in return.*

She hadn't wanted to believe Peter's hurtful accusations, but here she was experiencing all those awful sensations again. And she wasn't even supposed to be getting involved with anyone; she was here to work! Melissa thrust a pot into the sink and spoke without looking up. "I think you'd better go," she said, her voice shaking.

Stone lingered a moment before answering. "If that's how you want it."

Melissa nodded, but kept her face averted to hide the tears sliding down her cheeks. She heard the front door close behind him, then raised her teary gaze to the hand-painted sign above the kitchen sink. *Right,* she thought bitterly. *And, right again.* She felt a deep burning inside, searing like the hottest branding iron.

What was it about her that always pushed men away? Would Melissa forever be the victim of unrequited feelings? Was that to be her fate? Tears blistered down her cheeks, spilling into the soapy dishwater. What a fool she'd been to pin new hopes on Stone. Melissa had no business thinking about boyfriends at this time. She needed to rid her memory of old ones, and forget completely about "new" ones. As she'd astutely observed in the dining room, there clearly weren't any in the offing around here.

Chapter Sixteen

Stone trudged back toward his cabin, his hands shoved down into the pockets of his jeans. What a mess he'd made of everything. Might as well dub himself *Mister Smooth.* Stone had only been trying to flatter Melissa. Instead, he'd deeply insulted her somehow. He'd also apparently touched on a nerve. No. Make that two nerves. *Cross these off the list for future discussions: 1) Family history, and 2) Boyfriends.* That was, assuming there would even *be* any future discussions.

That Peter London guy had left Melissa really raw. But seriously. Could Stone be held accountable for that? Stone had known women like this before. If you were male, it was guilt by association. Didn't matter what kind of guy you were yourself. Stone sighed weightily, sorry the evening had taken its downward turn.

Everything had started out so hopefully. And boy, hadn't the discovery of that old Victrola been fun. To imagine it had been up in the attic all these years! That just showed how infrequently people went up there. Not that the Brandons bothered with the attic much. This wasn't even a second home for them; it was their fourth, as far as Stone understood. They principally

lived in Boston, but also had places on Nantucket and
in the Hamptons.

Over the years, the House at Homecoming Cove
had fallen to the bottom of their vacation-destination
list. Stone had heard the Brandons also enjoyed
traveling abroad and frequenting islands like the ones
where he used to work. While Stone had met his share
of wealthy people and viewed many as highly likable,
he found it hard to relate to their lifestyle day-to-day.
What Stone never could get over was the *why*. If they
had all that money, what made them choose to spend it
in the ways they did? Though many of the folks Stone
knew were philanthropists, an equal number were
simply careless with their cash. Spending fortunes on
lobster dinners at overpriced restaurants, for example,
when Stone knew firsthand that there was nothing finer
than fresh-caught blue crab.

This gave Stone an idea: a way to make things up
to Melissa. Though he'd obviously upset her, would she
really kick him out if he came bearing an apology and
offering food? So okay, he'd made a mistake and had
probably presumed too much. But he could say he was
sorry for that, couldn't he? Stone was man enough to
accept that Melissa wasn't interested in him in a serious
way. But he didn't want her hating him, either. Already,
they'd exchanged confidences, and had enjoyed a
shared discovery. What's more, they'd been physically
intimate. Even if Stone never held Melissa in his arms
again, he'd never erase the memory of her kiss.

Stone couldn't bear for things between them to end
badly. At the very least, Stone wanted Melissa to
remember him fondly as a friend. Stone didn't know
why Melissa's opinion of him mattered so much, but it
did. Stone might not have attended university or

worked in a high-gloss town, but he was a sensible sort with a good head on his shoulders. Plus, he was a good man.

Stone sulked into his cabin, realizing Melissa had hurt his pride. He was used to being judged as less capable than he was by outsiders. But when Melissa had done that, it had cut extra deep. It was like pouring salt on an old wound, though Stone didn't know why. In any case, he was determined to fix things. He owed it not just to himself but to the entire male population. Not all men were terrible jerks like Melissa's ex. Even if Stone accomplished nothing else during the rest of Melissa's stay here, he hoped he could help her see that.

Chapter Seventeen

Melissa stepped into the chilly morning air, finding frost coating the grass. She'd dressed quickly and had slipped into her jacket, determined to shut that banging garden gate. Its *whack, whack, whack*ing back and forth all night long had punctuated her sleep with fitful blasts of sound that hadn't quite woken her up, but had permeated her consciousness just the same. Gales ripped off the water, tossing her scarf back over her shoulder as she purposefully strode toward the garden. It was a shame that this piece of the property had fallen to rot, when the rest of it had been so nicely maintained. Well, most of it, she thought, remembering the disarray in the attic.

Melissa reached the gate and tugged it toward her, but it fought back as if bolstered by the wind. *Come on!* Melissa tugged harder. Then she leaned back in her boots and threw all her weight into her work. Finally, the gate flew forward, clanking loudly as its latch engaged, nearly knocking her off her feet. Melissa steadied herself, panting heavily, while thorny old rosebushes bowed toward her in the wind. She thought of the rose-painted sign above the kitchen window and experienced a deep-seated feeling of sadness. Or perhaps she was just feeling depressed over her ordeal last night.

She'd fallen into bed exhausted and had cried herself to sleep in a tearful heap. Melissa didn't know why she'd let Stone's joking upset her so badly, but she had. She supposed she hadn't healed from Peter as much as she'd hoped. But that was absurd, wasn't it? Letting a jerk like that still influence her experiences now? While Stone may have been insensitive, she finally got that he hadn't intentionally tried to hurt her. And if he'd suspected she'd developed a little thing for him, well then... He'd been absolutely right.

Melissa saw the misunderstanding that had transpired over dinner was much more her fault than Stone's. After the sweltering smog of the city, being with Stone had been like a breath of fresh air, and she'd been eager to draw him in. Probably too eager. That had been her undoing. Melissa was also far more fragile regarding her past than she'd guessed. Now that she realized it, she'd do well to tread cautiously where any future involvements were concerned. It would probably be best to steer clear of them altogether from now on.

Nonetheless, she needed to tell Stone she was sorry for the way she'd acted. She just needed to think up a way to frame her apology. Perhaps if she spent the day away from Homecoming Cove a solution would come to her. Melissa had been wanting to visit Port Scarborough. Now, the timing seemed ideal. She'd pour herself a travel mug of coffee and go explore the town.

When Stone arrived at the house later that morning to repair the attic vent covering, Melissa's SUV was missing from the drive. Perhaps she'd gone off to do an errand. Or maybe she'd used their misunderstanding as an excuse to run away. Not that Stone was really a guy worth running away from. Fact was, he didn't bite. He didn't even bark much most of the time. He was actually a fairly tame puppy. Stone frowned discontentedly and climbed from his truck, combating an unfamiliar sense of melancholy. It was ridiculous to miss a woman he barely knew, and yet he was disappointed to find Melissa gone. He'd hoped to see her straightaway and get things sorted out between them. Instead, he'd have to wait until later today, or maybe even sometime tomorrow, after she returned.

Stone hunched his shoulders and ambled forward, giving a perfunctory knock on the door. He knew Melissa wasn't home, but followed protocol just the same. Then he used the spare key Captain Bill had supplied him with and let himself into the house.

A little while later up in the attic, Stone heard a familiar sound and his heart lifted. It was Melissa playing the piano. Her sweet music drifted skyward, seeping through the floorboards below him and melodiously meeting his ears. Good. This was his chance to say he was sorry for whatever the heck she'd thought he'd done, and get on with a civil relationship. Stone set aside his work and started down the stairs, grateful Melissa had returned. Stone was a big believer in facing things head-on, rather than putting them off. Nothing good ever came of letting negative emotions fester.

He emerged in the parlor and looked curiously around. The old piano stood silent and its bench was empty, and yet the harmonious music played on. Stone glanced through the kitchen and into the living room. The Victrola, of course! He made his way in that direction, fully expecting to encounter Melissa. Perhaps she was relaxing in there or laying a fire for later that evening.

But when Stone stepped into the room he found it empty. The spinning record on the Victrola had reached the end of its track. The tonearm *scritch-scratch, scritch-scratch, scritch-scratch*ed back and forth, its needle bobbing up and down until it finally jumped over the deep groove and screeched across the label, smacking hard against the metal pin securing the record in place. Stone's heart nearly stopped. Slowly, he backed into the kitchen and then into the front foyer, where he peered out the window by the door.

Melissa's SUV had not returned.

Melissa spent the morning in Port Scarborough touring curio shops and hunting for hand-thrown pottery. She paused for lunch at a small Irish pub, where she ordered a steaming plate of fish and chips. Once fortified, she continued her excursions throughout the town, taking in the quaint harbor with its neat array of private boats and fishing vessels. After a while her feet grew tired and she decided to return to her temporary home. She stopped at a local doughnut shop first to pick up some fresh pastries to have for breakfast.

When Melissa pulled into the drive, she was surprised to spy a note taped to the front door. *Fixed the attic vent covering,* it said. *Sorry I missed you. Stone.* Melissa released a shaky breath, realizing she was sorry she'd missed him too. She'd really behaved badly last night, practically tossing Stone out on his ear, and not even bothering to listen when he'd tried to apologize. Well, now it was her turn to apologize. She'd tried to

put yesterday out of her mind, but the unfortunate turn
of events kept creeping back into her consciousness and
filling her with worry. The sooner she addressed things
with Stone, the better. She'd drop by his cabin
tomorrow evening and see if he was home.

Stone had been nothing but kind to her, and she'd
returned his caring with condemnation, a stark
bitterness that was subconsciously intended for another
man. It wouldn't be easy to explain this to Stone, but
Melissa felt she owed him that much. As a person and
as a...*friend*, she thought uneasily. At least she hoped
she and Stone could be friends—and that he'd forgive
her.

Chapter Eighteen

Later the next day, Melissa charged toward Stone's cabin holding a heaping plate of warm cookies. She was as nervous as she'd been during her audition at the conservatory from which she'd earned her degree. At least Melissa knew from his note that Stone was open to seeing her. She tentatively approached the cabin, seeing his truck was parked behind it, then stepped up onto the porch. Before she could knock, the door swung open. Stone stared down at her in stunned surprise.

"This is incredible," he said. "I was just coming to see you."

"You were?"

"Yes, I…" His eyes scanned hers, then focused on the covered plate in her hands. "You brought me something?" he asked, his expression warming.

"Homemade pumpkin spice," she offered cheerily. "I hope you'll like them."

"They're my favorite."

"I thought my spaghetti was your favorite?"

"Everything you make is my favorite." His voice was raspy and Melissa blushed.

Daylight was fading, tall stalks of wheat waving beyond the shimmering pond. "Why don't you come in?" Stone said. "I'll put some coffee on."

He ushered her through the door and closed it behind him. Melissa saw a bunch of pages spread out on his country kitchen table. They were very thin and had a faint blue cast. The drawings on them appeared to be mechanical, like architecture of some form. "Blueprints?" Melissa asked, setting her plate down beside them and unzipping her jacket.

Stone strode casually toward the table and folded them over. "Just a little project I'm working on."

"I had no idea you had architectural training," Melissa said, impressed.

"Don't," Stone answered. "But in high school I was mighty good at shop." He flashed her a humble grin. "Plus, I took an online course on building design while down in Saint Croix."

"Why there?"

"Hurricane season," Stone explained. "We were forced inland for two weeks. Figured I might as well do something productive with my time." He dropped his papers into the drawer of a bureau that stood beside a low wall, which served as a partition between the front half of the cabin and a modest bedroom, then slid it shut. Melissa spied the bottom portion of a double bed. She tried not to imagine Stone in it, forcing concentration on the topic at hand.

To think she'd envisioned Stone doing nothing but lying bare-chested in the sun and looking like a Greek god in the islands. Instead, he'd been studying architecture! Stone was full of surprises. Melissa swallowed hard, redirecting her thoughts. "Would you like me to help with the coffee?"

"Already on it," he said, walking to the small galley kitchen.

He scooped grounds into the coffee filter, his back to her. Melissa gathered her courage and forged ahead. "Stone, about last night…"

"No problem," he answered without turning. "I get it."

Melissa blinked, not expecting this response.

Stone set the coffee to brew, then leaned into the counter, bracing himself on both hands. "You're not interested in me in that way."

"No!"

Stone slowly turned around, his smoky gray gaze washing over her. "No?"

"I…" Melissa's heart beat faster. "I mean, I reacted badly. *Overreacted.* I threw a fit. I'm so sorry, Stone. I didn't mean to shut you out that way. It's just that the conversation reminded me of… Well, just something I didn't care to remember."

"You really sent me packing," he said, his expression pained.

"My feelings were hurt."

"*What?*"

"You were teasing me, and I was embarrassed." She stumbled on the words. "Embarrassed that I'd been so obvious that I…like you," she finished quickly before losing her nerve.

"You…?" he began, then broke out in disbelieving laughter. "Is that what your reaction was about?" His voice was thick with emotion. "You thought I'd rejected you?"

She scanned his eyes. "Well, didn't you?"

"Sweetheart," he said, and her heart fluttered. "I'm the one who delivered the line about new boyfriends." His voice was a soothing rumble as he took a step toward her. "Just how does that equal a rejection? You're the one who pushed me away, remember?"

Melissa's mind was a jumble and her heart was racing so fast she could scarcely breathe. "You weren't...mocking me?" she asked uncertainly.

"Mocking? Far from it. Melissa," he said, his voice husky. "I was *flirting* with you."

"Flirting?" she asked feebly, feeling the world tilt-a-whirl around her.

"It sounds like we've had a very big misunderstanding," Stone said, inching closer. "And hey, that's pretty good! Most couples date at least six weeks before having their first fight."

He shot her a crooked smile and heat flooded her face. Melissa felt mildly panicked and confused, yet mysteriously delighted at the same time. "I'd hardly say we're dating, Stone."

"You asked me to dinner," he replied without missing a beat.

"You were already there!"

"Tried to get me drunk and take advantage of me."

"Did not!"

"Made me carry you all the way from the dock into your house."

"Okay," she acquiesced, "maybe that part's true. But that was a few nights before."

"Doesn't negate that it happened."

Melissa tried to protest, feeling flustered. Was Stone saying what she thought he was? That he was equally attracted to her? "No, but..."

Stone devilishly lowered his eyebrows. "*And* you kissed me like a house on fire," he finished defiantly.

"You kissed me!" Melissa charged, feeling her face flame.

"I'd say it was mutual."

Melissa huffed, unsure whether she should laugh or scream. Stone was infuriating yet wonderful. Plus, he was amazingly interested in her. The coffeemaker beeped, signaling it was ready.

"Shall I pour us each a cup?" Stone asked, still grinning.

Melissa drew a sharp breath, feeling as winded as if she'd been on a crazy amusement park ride. "That would be great," she said, her heart beating wildly.

She sat at the table and unwrapped the cookie plate while Stone prepared their coffees, each with cream. When he sat across from her, she asked him, "Were you this much trouble in the Caribbean?"

"Most days I was far worse." He picked up one of her cookies and eyed it thoughtfully. "But not in the same way. I was never a problem for the ladies."

"Hmm. Somehow I doubt that," Melissa answered, guessing Stone had been a pretty big heartbreaker. "What was it like really, Stone?" she said, teasing. "A girl in every port?"

"Not all sailors are like that, you know." He took a bite of cookie and gave an appreciative sigh. "Totally delicious. Thank you."

"You're welcome," she said. "I'm glad you like them." Melissa shyly dipped her chin. "I brought them as a peace offering."

"Consider peace made," he said when she met his eyes. "Look, Melissa, we had a misunderstanding. One minute dinner was going great, and the next, things took a wrong turn. Neither of us meant to be hurtful to the other, I think we know that now."

"Thank you for being so gracious about it."

"Thank you for wanting to make amends," Stone answered. "It's much nicer being friends, wouldn't you say?" He stared at her deeply and she held her breath, hoping to goodness this was real. Melissa had never had a man look at her so completely. Like he totally saw who she was, and appreciated all of her.

"Yes," she said softly. "Much better."

Stone selected another cookie from the plate and smiled. "So? Where were you yesterday when I stopped by?"

"I went into Port Scarborough to see the town," she answered brightly.

"Did you like it?" Stone asked.

"It was quaint." She smiled, reliving her adventures. "And quiet."

"Everything around here's quiet," Stone answered, "except for during thunderstorms."

She selected a cookie for herself and took a nibble, washing it down with a sip of coffee. "So, why were you coming to see me?"

Stone appeared confounded a moment.

"Just now," she explained, "when I was about to knock on your door—"

Stone's face lit up. "Oh, yeah. That! I was coming to ask you over for Virginia blue crab."

"Blue crab?"

His eyes locked on hers and Melissa's heart stilled. "Consider it my peace offering. Dinner for two. I owe you one."

"When were you thinking of?" Melissa asked ridiculously, as if her calendar was full. Even if it were, Melissa knew that she would clear it in a heartbeat to share another meal with Stone.

"I have to stay late tomorrow and help Mac with something at the shop," he said. "But how about Saturday? Are you free?"

"I'll check my schedule," she said, her eyes never leaving his.

He waited a few seconds then queried, "And?"

Melissa couldn't keep from grinning. "You're in luck."

Stone leaned forward with a gravelly whisper. "Glad to hear it." Then he brushed his lips over hers. Melissa's head felt light and her pulse pounded fiercely as her body warmed from her cheeks to her toes. "Stone," she said in a breathy whisper.

"Hmm?" He leaned closer and softly kissed her again.

"Wha...what time...were you thinking of?"

Stone gave her firm peck on the lips, then sat back in his chair. "How about six?"

"Six will be fine," Melissa said weakly, grateful that she was sitting down.

"Good." Stone clinked his coffee mug against hers. "It's a date."

Chapter Nineteen

Melissa's whole body tingled all the way back to the farmhouse. After making their arrangements for Saturday, she had lingered a little longer, enjoying a second cup of coffee with Stone and hearing more about his exotic adventures at sea. He'd worked with some very interesting people and had some really funny stories to tell. In return, Stone had asked her about her music composing, and had listened earnestly as she described her new project and delineated a few of her past ones. While Melissa didn't often talk about her job, Stone's interest in her profession seemed genuine. Little by little, she'd found herself opening up to him, even sharing a few funny stories of her own about the characters she'd worked with, including celebrities and famed producers. In the end, she and Stone had decided that the folks he had crewed for and the people on Melissa's sets probably had a lot in common. They even joked that perhaps some of them were the same people! *I probably did have a few soap opera actors on board,* Stone had quipped. *There was certainly lots of drama!*

In the late afternoon hours, Melissa and Stone had bonded over coffee and cookies in a bubble of good humor and companionship that seemed easy. She'd thanked Stone for the coffee, and he'd said he appreciated the cookies, then he'd walked her to the door and accompanied her outside. When Stone had pulled her into his arms and said, *One for the road,* Melissa hadn't been able to refuse him. It had been a solitary kiss but a good one, deep and soulful with the promise of more kisses to come. Melissa's knees still trembled at the memory.

She made her way to the farmhouse as night closed in, grateful she'd left some lights on in the kitchen. Tonight, she'd go over some of yesterday's composition notes, then she'd take a bubble bath in the claw-foot tub upstairs and read herself to sleep in bed. Her heart felt light in the knowledge that she would see Stone again soon. Having that plan to look forward to on Saturday would make it so much easier to focus on her work beforehand. She was really making progress with her project now. Despite the oddities of this place, she thought, spying the farmhouse ahead of her in the shadows, Homecoming Cove was starting to grow on her. It was an interesting property with a fascinating history and more than a few surprises. The most surprising of all was a handsome sailor with come-hither gray eyes who was somehow working his way into her heart.

Melissa knew she was foolish to let herself fall for Stone, but—just for this moment—what could it hurt? Every woman deserved to know what it felt like to be admired and courted by a man like him. Who knew if Melissa would ever have the opportunity again? She had always been a planner and lived for tomorrow. For a change, she wanted to live for *today.* For, truthfully? One never really knew what the future might hold, or what it might be lacking. If Melissa never had another chance to be with someone like Stone, she wanted to experience that while she could.

Since arriving at Homecoming Cove, Melissa had felt freer than she ever had. It was like she'd finally been granted permission to fully be herself, and it felt marvelous. What's more, an incredible man like Stone seemed to appreciate her just as she was. What an awesome getaway this was turning out to be. It was as if the rest of the world had disappeared, and it was just her, and Stone, and her music, together at the Virginia Eastern Shore. What a lovely way to spend a working holiday, and what a wonderful break from New York City.

Chapter Twenty

Stone twisted violently under the covers, trying to get command of his ship in the storm. Gales gusted and sails swung back and forth in the crosswinds as icy rain pummeled the deck. His boat shoes slid on the glassy surface just as the boom came around. Then *wham*, Stone was rammed in the shoulder with what felt like a steel helmet and he went flying overboard, diving headlong for the sea that rose and fell in angry whitecaps all around him. Stone gulped in air, but he couldn't breathe. His lungs had filled with water. Then he was sinking down…down…down…a fine golden chain flitting just out of reach, floating above him in the water. Stone opened his eyes and jerked into a sitting position, clutching his sides. He choked and gasped, his breathing heavy, as he slowly got his bearings in the room. That's when he heard the music.

Melissa set her feet on the floor, her head foggy. It was still Friday, wasn't it? She'd worked a full and productive day, and tomorrow evening she'd be seeing Stone. But her deep slumber had been disturbed only seconds ago. She'd been awakened by a haunting tune. But how on earth could that be? She sat on the edge of the bed, her eyes adjusting to the dim light. Moonlight angled through the windows, stretching out across the carpet and shimmering against the hardwood floor. It was the middle of the night, and yet she'd heard it. *Someone was in the house playing the piano downstairs.* Melissa shakily got to her feet, glancing around for something—anything—to take with her. She settled for the hefty flashlight that sat on her nightstand. Captain Bill had left it for her in the kitchen that first day, along with a note suggesting she keep it by her bedside for emergencies. Of course, he'd been thinking of the house losing power during a storm. Not of something like this.

Melissa laid a trembling hand on the doorknob and pulled open the door leading to the hall. Music spilled up the stairs and curved around toward her room, nearly blasting her with its force. She didn't know whether she should call out or try to catch the intruder unawares. Deciding the element of surprise might work in her favor, she opted to creep down the stairs, grimacing tightly as each one creaked. Though surely no one could hear her above the loud torrents of music. Fear coursed through her veins, but Melissa propelled herself onward. She needed to confront it, lest it confront her first. She descended the final riser and inched toward the parlor as music crashed toward her in sonic waves. Melissa's mouth felt dry and her heart struck violently against her rib cage, slamming like a jackhammer. She stepped around the corner with her flashlight raised, preparing to defend herself. Melissa's heart rose in her throat. The room was empty and the piano was still. Yet the music cascaded forward from another room. *The Victrola!*

Melissa raced through the kitchen and into the living room, beholding the eerie sight: the old record player spinning around and around, as music poured from its fluted horn.

Moonlight glinted on the cove outside as the flashlight dropped from Melissa's grasp. Then she raced for the porch and out the back door, and tore like a madwoman for Stone's cabin.

Chapter Twenty-One

Stone was still in a daze when the rapid pounding sounded at his door. "Stone! Stone! Open up!" The voice was breathless, full of fear. *Melissa.*

Stone sprang from his bed and rushed to the door, yanking it open. Melissa stood there pallid in the moonlight, the blood drained from her face. She wore nothing but a long T-shirt that draped toward her knees, hitting her legs mid-thigh. She pushed shaking fingers through her hair and stared up at him with panicked blue eyes. "The Victrola!" she said, still huffing and puffing from her dash through the farm. "It was playing!"

Stone brought his arms around her. "By itself?" he asked, searching her eyes. She nodded, her lips trembling, and Stone felt a jolt inside. That sounded just like what had happened to him on Wednesday morning. When he'd come across the spinning record, he'd tried to dismiss it as a fluke. He told himself that perhaps Melissa had cranked the old record player just before leaving on her trip into town, seconds before he got there—though rationally Stone knew none of that made sense. He hadn't heard anything when he'd first arrived to repair the vent covering. He hadn't even noticed the music until he'd been working in the attic.

"There must be some explanation," he said as they stood on the stoop.

"There is no explanation," she said, her expression solemn.

"Something must have knocked it, gotten it started…"

"Yes, but what?" Her voice was shrill. "Stone," she said, after a lull, "I didn't want to believe this, but maybe…"

"No," he said firmly. "That's impossible."

"How do we know what is and *isn't* possible in this world?"

"*In this world,* Melissa. Exactly."

She blinked and Stone feared he'd been too brash. Just look at her. She was scared out of her wits. "I'm sorry," he whispered hoarsely. "I didn't mean to sound harsh." He released his embrace and draped an arm around her shoulder. "Come on, let's get you indoors."

Stone led her into the cabin and to the compact love seat that sat before the woodstove. He eased her down onto its cushions, then held both her hands. "Want something to drink?"

"Yeah," she said, staring ahead at some point right in the middle of his chest. But it wasn't like she was looking at his undershirt at all. It was like she was gazing at nothing.

"How about some tea?"

"Got anything stronger?" she said, still oddly transfixed.

"Whiskey?"

Melissa nodded, and Stone reluctantly released her hands to go and pour it. He had a simple but purposeful bar, and it was well stocked. He poured them each a shot, then came to join her on the love seat.

"It was so weird, Stone," she muttered softly. He handed her a glass and she took it. "And loud, I mean *really* loud."

"I know, I—"

She sharply met his gaze. "You heard it too, didn't you? And not just tonight; you've heard it before."

Stone's knuckles went white as he gripped his glass. "Piano music, yes. But I thought that was you."

Melissa vehemently shook her head. "I never play after dinner."

"*Never?*"

"It's work for me, Stone. Since I work from home, I decided long ago that I needed to set regular hours. If I didn't, I'd go mad—composing all night long. Even if I have to eat late, I set mealtime as my limit. Once I sit down to dinner, I'm done for the day."

Stone took a slug of his whiskey and Melissa followed suit. "That must take a lot of discipline."

"Not as much as you might think. It's become a routine to me now. At least it was one before…"

"Before what?" Stone asked gently.

Melissa grabbed a throw blanket off the arm of a nearby chair to cover her legs. Stone saw they were prickled with goose bumps and that her feet looked raw from her sprint across the grass. "May I?"

"Of course," he said, briefly setting down his glass to help her spread the blanket across her knees.

Melissa took another swallow of whiskey before answering his question. "Before I came to Homecoming Cove, I went through a bad spell. Couldn't compose at all for a while."

"I'm sorry," he said sympathetically. "Did this have to do with—?"

"Yes," she said. "With him. Although it shouldn't have." She took another sip of her drink, rolling it over her tongue. "Maybe it was him, maybe it was other things. Maybe I was ready for a break. I don't know." She studied the pattern of the hooked rug on the cabin floor, then looked up. "The truth is, I was pushing myself very hard. To the point where I was almost ready to break."

"Oh, Melissa." Stone laid his hand on the one she had resting in her lap.

"I know it was crazy," she continued. "But I felt like I had to do everything one hundred percent well, all the time. I never turned down a job, because I feared I couldn't. If I let one opportunity pass, then someone else might pick it up. Then that someone else might get called first next time."

"You don't have to tell me any of this."

"I know." She gave a pained smile. "But I want to, feel like I finally need to tell it to someone."

Stone watched her encouragingly.

Melissa drew in a breath, paused, then released it. "I feared I was having a breakdown." Her voice warbled as her eyes filled with tears. "Maybe I already have."

The glass shook in her hand and Stone quickly set it aside. Melissa folded her face in her hands and let out a sob. "It's happened, hasn't it?" she asked plaintively. "I've lost my mind!"

"No." Stone's reply was steady and immediate. "You haven't lost it at all. You're no crazier than I am."

She looked up at him and tears streamed down her face. "Then maybe we're both insane."

Stone reached out and trailed a thumb down her cheek, tracing the moisture there. "You're a beautiful, intelligent woman," he said soothingly, "who's encountered a shock. Maybe you were under strain when you got here. And maybe some of the things you've experienced at Homecoming Cove have made it worse. Maybe even you and I shouldn't have—"

"No!" She reached for his hand and held on tight. "You're one of the good things." His features relaxed as she gazed at him. "The *best thing* that's happened to me in a long while, either at—or away from—Homecoming Cove.

Stone shared a shaky smile. "Hope so."

"Know so," she said, tightly gripping his hand.

"Melissa," he said, his voice taking on a deeper timbre. "I don't know what happened with that record player, but you're right, I heard it too. So if they're going to toss one of us in the loony bin, they might as well take two for the price of one and throw away the key."

Melissa laughed, her spirits brightening. No matter what was going on, at least she wasn't facing it alone. She had Stone in her corner. "Maybe tomorrow this will all seem like a bad dream," she said. "We'll convince ourselves we only imagined it."

"Maybe," he said, sounding unconvinced. Stone put his arm around her shoulder and nestled her under the crook of his arm. Melissa sighed and leaned against him, feeling warm, comfortable, and safe, as if nothing in the world could touch her. It seemed like it couldn't, as long as she was with Stone. Melissa didn't know what had gone on with the Victrola, but she had a sinking feeling they shouldn't have removed it from the attic. Without in any way intending to, she and Stone had disturbed things somehow. Tempted fate.

Melissa reached for her glass and they each sipped from their drinks in silence. Eventually, Stone said, "Maybe we should put the Victrola back in the attic."

"That's just what I was thinking," Melissa agreed.

"It's obviously broken," he continued.

"Obviously."

"Maybe we should have left it in place."

"Yes."

"Melissa?"

"Hmm?"

"I'm starting to worry about you being here."

She pushed back in his embrace to meet his eyes. "What do you mean?"

"If that first night on the dock wasn't enough to warn you away, maybe this latest episode should be."

Her face sagged with comprehension. "You want me to go?" she asked, unable to mask the hurt in her voice.

"You know that I don't." Stone viewed her with concern. "But Melissa, I can't bear the thought of anything happening to you." He searched her eyes. "What if the vent covering in the attic coming loose wasn't an accident?"

"But that's ridiculous. I wasn't even there!"

"No. But something else could occur."

"Like what, Stone? I can hardly see how I was in jeopardy from music playing."

"Think back to the dock, Melissa." She did and shuddered in his arms. "You said you'd been awakened by music. And that you'd felt pulled to the water. What if I hadn't been there? What if I hadn't shown up exactly when I did?"

"But you did! You did show up! And why?"

Stone's gray eyes lit with understanding. "Because I heard the music too…" His voice trailed off.

"Somehow music is the key," she said.

"None of this makes any sense. It's just like those stupid dreams."

"What dreams?"

"It's not important."

"Please, Stone." She stared at him beseechingly. "I want to know."

Stone studied her in silence. She was right. He should tell her. Stone didn't know that his dreams were connected to what was going on now, but he couldn't prove that that weren't, either. "All right. I'll tell you. But I've got to warn you, the dream is a little dark." Stone threw back the rest of his whiskey and set down his glass. Then he told Melissa about the recurring nightmare he'd had for the past twenty years. Melissa listened silently, caught up in Stone's horror as he described the feeling of drowning again and again.

She tenderly took his hand.

"And there's always been that chain dangling above you in the water?"

Stone nodded.

"What do you think it is?"

"I've never been sure. For a time I thought it was the chain to a pocket watch. But right when I'm about to reach it—when it's finally within my grasp—the dream ends and I wake up."

"When did all this start?"

His skin was as pale as if he'd died a million deaths just in the telling. "Years ago. I think I must have been about eight years old."

"Eight?" she questioned. "That's very precise. Did something happen around that time? Something traumatic?"

Stone shook his head. "My childhood was pretty tame. I didn't really experience much trauma until I lost my folks. Then there was that episode in the Caribbean."

Melissa gasped. "You don't mean...?"

Stone stared at her. "I experienced something very similar to what happened in those dreams. It was like déjà vu all over again."

"That must have been terrifying."

Stone affected a laugh. "You won't see me getting out on the water today."

"Nobody would blame you," Melissa answered. She brought her hand to her chin and looked at him thoughtfully. "Eight," she said aloud, mulling it over. "What grade were you in?"

Stone shrugged. "Third, I guess."

"And nothing memorable happened that year?"

"Memorable?" Stone released her hand and stretched his arms above him, settling them behind his head. For a long while he stared at the ceiling, seeming to examine every knot in the wood of the exposed beams. Finally, he said, as if remembering, "I've got a sad recollection from then, but it's not exactly traumatic."

Melissa stared at him expectantly.

"My Grandma Jocelyn died," he said. "She's the one who was married to Captain Bill."

"I'm sorry. Were you close?"

"Fairly, yeah. But as far as I know, her passing was peaceful."

"What did she die of?"

"My folks told me 'old age.' Later I pieced together that it must have been cancer."

Melissa slowly shook her head. "You're right. That hardly seems connected to—"

Stone exhaled sharply, then surprised her by shouting, "The box!"

His eyes spoke volumes, as if he was putting all sorts of things together. "It was a keepsake box, one that had been in the family for generations. When my grandmother passed, my dad wanted me to have it as the last remaining male heir from the Stone side."

Melissa's heart pounded with excitement. "What's in it?"

Chapter Twenty-Two

A few minutes later, Stone dragged what looked like a cross between an old steamer trunk and a small pirate's chest out of the corner. He carried it across the room and set it on the coffee table before Melissa, springing open its locks. A wealth of musty old memorabilia nested inside: a leather-bound captain's log, an antique spyglass, an old service revolver... Stone shifted some of the items aside and reached down into the bottom of the container. "This is what I was looking for," he said, carefully removing a small hand-carved box from beneath the heap of precious objects.

Melissa stared in awe at the wealth of collectibles in the trunk and then at the carved box in Stone's hand.

He removed the box's lid and carefully set it down. Then, with very nimble fingers, he plucked up the delicate gold necklace chain and displayed it in the air. A shiny heart-shaped locket dangled from it.

"Melissa," he said with assurance. "The chain in my dreams... I think it might have belonged to this."

She gasped at the locket's surprising beauty. "Whose was it?"

"I'm pretty sure it belonged to Fiona." He dropped the locket into Melissa's outstretched palm and its lightweight chain coiled silkily around it, sending a shiver up her arm.

"Check the initials on the back," Stone urged.

Melissa gingerly flipped it over. "F. H." Her mouth dropped open. "Fiona Henderson."

"All this talk about Fiona and her music, it got me thinking… Then, in retelling the dream, everything came together."

"She must have given it to Lewis," Melissa said. "Is there a picture inside?"

Stone blinked at her like he hadn't expected the question.

"Sometimes these old lockets…" She ran the tip of her forefinger along the locket's outer edge, looking for the clasp. "Yes, here it is." She pressed in the tiny post and the locket clicked open.

Stone's jaw unhinged. "Wow."

Melissa studied the faded black-and-white photo, just making it out. "It's a baby!" she cried with delight. "A little girl!"

"That must have been Fiona," Stone answered. "As an infant."

"Yes," Melissa said thoughtfully. "Who else could it be?" She closed the locket and handed it back to Stone.

"What I don't get," he said, "is how this worked its way into my dreams."

"You must have seen it at some point."

"Of course. When I received the box, I went through everything in it in detail. Later, when I went to live with my grandparents in Port Scarborough, I chronicled its contents again, sharing each piece with Captain Bill. Though my Grandma Jocelyn had shown him these items years before, he still pretended to be highly interested."

"He probably was. What a treasure trove of family history you've got there."

Stone pondered the locket a moment before speaking. "I suppose the locket was just a random detail that got woven into my underwater story. Who knows why the subconscious mind connects things the way it does. Dreams are nebulous that way sometimes."

"Oftentimes," Melissa asserted.

Stone tucked the locket away in its box, then returned it to the bottom of the trunk. As he did, he lifted the captain's log in his other hand to move it out of the way. Melissa spied the corner of something peeking out from between its closed pages.

"Do you mind?" she asked him, and Stone nimbly passed it to her.

Melissa pried open the book to the page where an item had been slipped inside. It was another black-and-white photograph, this time of a stunning woman with hair piled high in a Gibson girl style and pretty pale eyes. Melissa looked at Stone. "Fiona?"

He nodded. "As an adult." Stone gently took the old photo from her hand and examined it closely. "You know," he said, looking up, "Captain Bill was right. She does favor you." He stopped himself. "Or vice versa."

Melissa stared down at the picture again. It wasn't an identical likeness by any means, but there did seem to be a faint resemblance. "Hmm, maybe a little, but I'd hardly call it earthshattering."

Stone's eyes danced with mischief. "Maybe if you did your hair like hers…?"

"Stop," she said, laughing. "That style's so yesterday."

Stone smiled, obviously enjoying her company and their conversation.

Melissa glanced down at the captain's log in her hands, scanning through a couple of pages. The old wood-pulp paper had yellowed and was brittle to the touch, but the penmanship of its entries remained sharp and clear. Each page appeared filled with notations, map coordinates, weather conditions, and other navigational details. "Did this belong to Lewis?" she asked.

Stone nodded. "He left a couple of others like it behind. They're in the bottom of the trunk. His last log went down with his ship."

Melissa frowned and handed the book back to Stone. "At least you still have these things of his."

"Yeah, and other things that have belonged to the family. Though Lewis was the original owner of the box, other descendants added to it over the years by including their special keepsakes."

Stone tucked Fiona's photograph back inside the old captain's log and also put that away, locking up the trunk.

"It's really quite incredible," Melissa said, "that your family has managed to save all those things for so many years." Her head still reeled. She'd seen Fiona! The one who had owned the piano and played music in the house. *Maybe the one who's still making music in the house,* she thought with alarm. But why?

Had she and Stone somehow disturbed Fiona's spiritual slumber? Was it because Melissa—a blond musician composing songs at Fiona's keyboard—had reminded Fiona of herself? Then another, darker thought occurred. What if Fiona wasn't focused on building a connection with Melissa, but rather saw her as a rival? An earthly being who'd captured the attention, and affections, of Lewis's last remaining heir? Was it possible that in her twisted misery Fiona wanted Stone all to herself? Melissa recalled her sudden awakening on the dock, and felt herself shiver. What if Stone was right? What if Melissa really was in danger at Homecoming Cove?

Stone's steady voice pulled her out of her reverie. "That's what I'm planning to do, you know." Melissa suddenly realized he'd been talking and she'd missed something. "Donate them to the mariner's museum."

"There's a mariner's museum around here?" she asked, reengaging in the conversation.

"Not yet." Stone shared a confident grin. "But someday."

Melissa put the pieces of the puzzle together, pleasantly surprised. Stone had just revealed his hidden ambition. How cool. "The blueprints! Your plan?"

"What better way to preserve history?"

"I love history," Melissa admitted. "Some might call me a bit of a history nerd."

"What, you?" he said teasingly.

"Seriously. I've got my family's history mapped all the way back. Family crests and everything."

"Impressive."

"Hardly as impressive as what you've got in there," she said, indicating the trunk.

"I hope you'll come to visit," Stone said. "Be there for the grand opening?"

"Will we crack a bottle of champagne against the side of the building?"

"You betcha," Stone said, and they both laughed.

Suddenly it was hard for Melissa to imagine that she had felt terrified only a short time ago. "Stone…?" she ventured carefully, lest Stone think she'd become completely unglued. "About Fiona's locket…and those things that have been happening at the house…? Do you think that maybe it's possible Fiona's restless?"

To her relief he didn't make light of her question. "Restless? I don't know."

"She and Lewis did come to a terrible end."

"Agreed."

Melissa stared at the trunk, then spoke wistfully. "You'd think Fiona would be at peace now that she and Lewis are finally together."

"Maybe they aren't." Despite the absurdity of the topic, Stone's assertion sounded reasonable. "It could be that something prevented that."

Melissa felt a slight tug on her heartstrings. "How sad that would be if Lewis and Fiona not only lost each other on earth, but were also unable to find each in the hereafter. That would make their story a double tragedy."

Stone frowned. "You're right."

Melissa wasn't sure whether it was the effects of the whiskey or the fright she'd experienced earlier, but suddenly she felt drained.

Stone studied her a beat, then said, "You must be exhausted. Come on." He held out his hand and she took it, her eyes questioning.

"Where are we going?"

"You need sleep and I do too," Stone stated unequivocally. "Both of us have work to do tomorrow."

He pulled her to her feet and she began to protest. The last thing Melissa wanted to do tonight was go back to the farmhouse alone.

"You're tired, I'm tired…" Stone said, cutting her off before she could speak. "And the love seat is way too small for either of us."

He tugged her toward his bed, switching off lights as he went, and Melissa felt heat seep through her body. "Stone, I…"

"We're just going to sleep, all right?" he said, folding back the covers. Stone sat on the bed and pulled her to him until the hem of her T-shirt met his bare knees. In his plain white undershirt and camp shorts, Stone looked as sexy as sin. But Melissa wasn't ready for anything more, and somehow he sensed it. Perhaps neither was he.

"I'd never hurt you, Melissa," he said, easing her down beside him. "And I'd never make love to you if I knew you were going away." He leaned toward her. "Because once we'd done that…" He pushed back her hair and his lips met her neck. Goose bumps skittered across her skin and Melissa released a ragged breath. "I'd never be able to leave you," he whispered. "Not ever." Stone supported her in his arms and lowered her onto the mattress, gently laying her head on the pillow.

"Good night, my sweet," he said, with a feathery soft kiss. "Pleasant dreams."

Stone settled himself down behind her, drawing the covers around them. Then he held her close, the warmth of his body pressed to hers, while her cheeks burned hot and her heart raced out of control, beating wildly in his strong embrace.

Chapter Twenty-Three

Melissa stirred drowsily, delighted to find herself cradled in Stone's arms. What a warm, wonderful feeling it was. He shifted behind her and stroked her hair. "You awake?" he asked, sounding groggy.

Melissa happily studied the pattern the sunlight cast across the kitchen table. "Yeah, how about you?"

"Nope. I'm sleeping," he teased. He playfully jostled her in his arms. "And sleep-talking."

"Ha-ha," she said, speaking over her shoulder. Her stomach rumbled, and she was surprised by how famished she felt. The excitement of last night must have kicked her metabolism into overdrive. "You hungry?"

"A little."

"A *little*?" she answered with a laugh. "I'm starved!" Melissa slowly sat up and turned toward him. He looked adorably disheveled with his morning stubble and his hair all a mess. "How about a big country breakfast?"

He stared at her, squinty-eyed. "I'm afraid I don't have eggs and bacon."

Melissa grinned triumphantly. "You might not, but I do."

"Does this mean I'm invited?" he asked with a lazy grin.

"Yeah," she said, smiling down at him. "Besides, I need a bodyguard."

Stone sat up partway, leaning back on his elbows. "Bodyguard?"

"I'd probably feel a lot better going back in the farmhouse if I'm not alone. I mean, at least not initially. Until I'm sure that darned Victrola has stopped playing."

Stone laughed and sent her a captain's salute. "Aye, aye!" he said, gray eyes twinkling. "I accept the job."

Melissa waited on the porch while Stone changed into jeans and a sweater. He emerged from the cabin carrying the throw blanket with him. "Why don't you wrap up in this while we head back?" he asked her. "There's still frost on the grass."

Melissa viewed the icy green blades glistening in the sunlight and tugged the blanket around her shoulders. "You're right," she said frowning. "My feet will freeze."

"Oh, no, they won't," Stone said with a sudden thought. Then, before she could stop him, he scooped her up into his arms and stepped down off the stoop.

"Stone!" she protested giddily, kicking her bare feet in the air. "You can't make a habit of this!"

He cocked an eyebrow and forged ahead toward the path. "Can't I?"

When Stone rounded the corner he stopped in his tracks.

Captain Bill stood by his truck, staring straight at the couple.

"Captain Bill!" Melissa cried with surprise.

He eyed them both in an appraising fashion, then cut Stone a steely glance. "Morning."

Stone shot his grandpa a warning look. "We weren't expecting you."

Bill frowned with disapproval. "That's what I gathered."

"What are you doing here?" Stone asked, still holding Melissa.

"Came to check on that attic vent covering you mentioned coming loose."

"Already took care of it."

"Appears you've been busy," Bill said, and Melissa flushed from her head to her bare toes.

She glanced uncertainly at Stone. "Maybe we should—?"

"Yeah," Stone said. "Let me carry you over to the patio, and you can wait for me on the porch."

"Sounds like a good idea," Bill said to Melissa. "I'd like a word with my grandson."

Stone deposited Melissa on the patio and stormed back toward his granddad with an angry scowl. "You had no right insinuating what you did," he said under his breath.

"Didn't have to insinuate. It was obvious."

"Not as obvious as you think."

"Just look at what she's wearing—and not."

"I'm perfectly aware of what Melissa's wearing—and not," Stone replied testily. "I'm a grown man, Grandpa."

"Then act like it," Bill said, "and not some silly teenage boy high on hormones. Melissa Carter is a renter here, a paying guest. You'd do well to remember that, and not go taking advantage of the immediate situation."

"I haven't taken advantage of anything," Stone said, fuming. "Not that it would be any business of yours if I had."

Bill glanced at the porch, then shot Stone a weighty look. "We'll sort this later," he said, plowing back toward his truck. "Now's not the time."

"Grandpa!" Stone called.

But it was already too late. Bill had climbed into the cab and slammed the door shut.

Stone trudged back toward Melissa as Bill's truck rumbled away. Stone was embarrassed by his grandfather's behavior. He knew how it had looked when Captain Bill saw them, but his demeanor toward them—and especially Melissa—had been nothing short of rude.

Stone pulled back the screen door and it creaked noisily. "I'm sorry about Captain Bill," he said, staring down at Melissa as she sat in a chair, his throw blanket still snug around her shoulders. "He didn't have the right to assume...to say the things he did. I apologize."

"It's okay," she told him. "I can only imagine what he thought."

"I'll straighten things out later," Stone assured her. He glanced through the glass-paneled door that led to the living room. Through it, he spied the old Victrola, which appeared perfectly still. "Hear anything?" he asked Melissa.

"Not a sound."

"Maybe things have calmed down."

He opened the door for Melissa and she stood and walked through it. With the morning sunlight coming through the windows, the living room appeared perfectly peaceful and inviting. They both approached the old record player and studied it from either side. Nothing looked different from the last time Melissa had seen it—only this time it wasn't playing music. Stone lifted the single disc from the Victrola and tucked it away with the rest of the collection in the series box.

"Shall I put these things back in the attic?" Stone asked her.

"I think that's probably a good idea, don't you?"

"Why don't I take care of that while you go and slip some clothes on? Then you and I can make breakfast together."

She smiled at him in surprise. "You're offering to help?"

"I make an awfully mean omelet," he said with a grin.

"I'll make the bacon and the coffee," she offered happily.

"It's a deal."

Chapter Twenty-Four

Stone returned the album box to its previous spot in the attic, then hefted the Victrola up the attic stairs. It wasn't too heavy for him to carry by any means— simply awkward. He took care with its bulky form, steering the huge horn away from either wall as he climbed the steps. He cleared the top stair and carried the old record player to the corner beside the album box. Its covering tarp was still folded on top of a stack of boxes where Melissa had left it. He set the Victrola down gently, then shook out the tarp and positioned it carefully over its edges. As he did, he felt a sharp blast of air. A shiver tore down Stone's spine and he straightened in alarm, feeling frozen all over. It was as if he'd been dumped into the cold North Atlantic in the dead of winter, and without warning. Stone stood there shivering and wrapped his arms around himself, swiftly massaging the tops of his arms through his sweater sleeves. What on earth had just happened?

Stone's gaze panned the room, taking everything in—from the neatly arranged clutter to the recently repaired attic vent covering. Fine particles of dust danced through the air, twirling like miniature ballerinas. His countenance slowly warmed, his blood pumping hard to raise his body temperature to its normal state. Stone stared down at his fingertips, noting they'd nearly turned blue. Stone was immediately consumed by a sense of dread concerning Melissa. He couldn't let her stay in this house. Something was clearly going on. Something that neither of them could logically explain. Though Stone suspected Melissa was right: it had something to do with Fiona. And if Fiona had loved Lewis all those years ago, then perhaps she was somehow distantly aware that Stone was a part of him. Stone shared Lewis's genes and was his last living heir. Stone broke out in a sweat, pondering what this could mean for Melissa.

Stone had been looking after these grounds for the past eight months and had never experienced any odd disturbances until Melissa's arrival. Perhaps there had been some sort of equilibrium then, with Stone and whatever was left of Fiona occupying the property. Whether it was Fiona's spirit or simply some sort of spiritual imprint she'd left in place due to her tragic experiences here, Stone didn't know. He could barely stand to believe he was contemplating such lunacy as real. Stone's heart thumped harder at the deeper understanding that Melissa's well-being—maybe even her life—was in jeopardy. Stone's ardor for her had been so apparent, and perhaps these walls had ears— and eyes. Stone had been drawn to Melissa from the very start. Could it be Fiona was jealous…? That she wanted Stone all to herself and was trying to send messages through her music? Messages to draw Stone in, and push Melissa away? Or worse, get rid of Melissa permanently?

Stone shook his head, thinking he couldn't possibly be getting this right. He was taking leaps of logic, imagining impossible scenarios. But then why did he feel a growing sense of concern over Melissa's safety? Stone realized he was boiling now, overheating in his sweater. In a matter of minutes he'd gone from freezing cold to practically on fire. Stone shoved up his sweater sleeves and made his way quickly out of the attic. He'd been too long in putting the Victrola away. Melissa would be missing him downstairs. He reached the upstairs hall and turned to close the attic door. But before he could lay his hand on its knob it forcefully banged shut as if someone had pulled it closed from the inside. Stone stood staring at the doorknob as seconds ticked by, and his pulse pounded in his ears. It had to be the wind, acting as a vacuum. But with the attic vent covering repaired, where would any gust of wind have come from?

"Everything all right up there?" Melissa called from the base of the stairs.

"Fine!" Stone shouted back to her. "Coming right down!"

Melissa sat at the dining room table watching Stone toy with his omelet. Either he wasn't hungry or something was bothering him, because the food was absolutely delicious. By the time Stone had returned from the attic, she'd brewed the coffee and the bacon was well under way. It took Stone less than ten minutes to whip together a fabulous omelet made from sautéed onions, green peppers, mushrooms, eggs, and cheddar cheese. He'd topped it with a dollop of sour cream and a spoonful of salsa for flair. It was almost like a new twist on huevos rancheros, and Melissa was very impressed.

Stone set down his fork and picked up his coffee mug. "So what do you have planned for today?" he asked her.

She'd actually been thinking about that while she'd been busy by herself in the kitchen. "I'm hoping to finish up my project," Melissa said optimistically.

"Finish?" he asked. "That's great."

Melissa nibbled on her last piece of bacon, polishing it off. "Yeah, I've been pretty pleased with my progress. I'm on the last twenty pages of the script. So, if everything goes well—"

"Melissa," he said, startling her. "There's something I need to tell you." His normally pleasant features had a dark cast.

"Yes, Stone?"

"The more I think about it, the more I believe you should leave Homecoming Cove."

Melissa sat there, unable to immediately respond. This was the second time Stone had mentioned this. While she knew Stone spoke out of concern for her, it still hurt her feelings that he'd want her to go. Sure, some weird things had happened here. But there were probably logical ways to explain them all. Just think of that wavering curtain by the window that Melissa had foolishly mistaken for a ghost! And all on account of a blast of air from the floor vent. While the old Victrola playing on its own had seemed spooky, couldn't there also be a reasonable way to explain that? Perhaps the crank had been overwound, then gotten stuck, and suddenly released itself. Or maybe they'd experienced slight earth tremors here, something like a spate of low-grade earthquakes—might those have set the turntable spinning somehow? Melissa stopped herself, realizing she was reaching for straws.

"I understand that you're worried," she finally said.

He leaned forward and latched onto her arm. "Not just worried, Melissa. I'm afraid for your safety."

She set down her coffee and stared at him.

"I would never forgive myself if something happened to you."

"What makes you think anything's going to?"

"You nearly drowned your second night here!"

"I was sleepwalking, Stone. Overwrought. Still keyed up from all the pressure I'd been under in New York. I didn't mention this before, but I used to sleepwalk as a child, particularly when I was under stress. It didn't happen often, but—"

"Did you ever walk out of the house?"

"What?"

"Did you ever go outdoors, Melissa?"

"Well, no. Of course not. At least, I don't think so. My parents would have told me."

"So then," Stone pressed, not relenting. "Why did that happen here? Why not just walk into another bedroom, or downstairs into the kitchen? Why out onto the dock—in the middle of the night—when the water was freezing?"

Melissa heaved a breath. "I don't know. I haven't analyzed it that far."

"Well, maybe you should. Maybe we both should," he said seriously.

"I'd been dreaming," she replied plaintively. "About the cove and a ship returning."

"Whose ship?"

"I don't know; it was very old."

"You were dreaming about Lewis and Fiona," he stated, as if it was a fact.

"Maybe. I mean, I suppose that makes sense. I'd been pondering Captain Bill's story, thinking about it all day."

"Maybe in your dream, you thought *you were* Fiona."

"Stone."

"Or maybe," he added more darkly. "Fiona wanted you to think that, and was leading you."

"To where?"

"To harm!"

Melissa defiantly met Stone's gaze. She might have been out of sorts last night, but now in the light of day she'd been able to put things into perspective. She was in an old house with a spooky old legend. A few natural phenomena had occurred and she'd let her imagination get the better of her. Maybe she and Stone shouldn't have messed with the past and brought down that old Victrola. But it was safely back in the attic. No real damage had been done. "I don't want to go. I like it here. What's more, I'm finally able to work. You don't know how it was in New York. I was blocked. *Blocked*, do you hear me? I couldn't work for weeks on end; it was devastating. But here…" She stared wistfully out the back window at the barn and the garden and the glistening cove with fall foliage fluttering around it. "*Here*, I'm able to be myself. I feel in touch. Completely connected to my creative self. I don't know how to explain it any better than that." Besides feeling connected to herself, Melissa was also starting to feel a deep connection with Stone, though she wasn't quite brave enough to say so. Last night had felt like heaven, sleeping in his arms.

Stone hung his head. "You've got to believe I don't want you to leave."

Melissa reached across the table and took his hand. "Then don't let me."

Stone looked up, appearing resigned. "I wish I didn't have to go in today, but I've got a full slate."

"Of course you should go in." She tightened her hold on his hand. "We each need to continue with our lives. We can't let some old story, or silly superstition—"

"I'll do whatever you want," he said, cutting her off. "Play it your way. But don't think I won't be sticking close."

Melissa smiled softly. "That's what I'm counting on."

Stone paused briefly, then began anew. "So!" he said. "Are we still on for dinner?"

"I'm looking forward to that crab."

"Great. I'll pick up two dozen steamed on my way home." The way he'd said it, it was almost as if they were already living together as a couple. Melissa tried to imagine what that might be like, just her and Stone living in this grand old house on the Eastern Shore, and little tickles of delight danced through her. She could see them standing on the dock, Stone with his arm around her as the dusk tucked in the day. It was like the two of them belonged here.

"You do like potatoes?" Stone asked, and Melissa realized she'd missed something. "To go with the steamed crab," he continued. "Boiled potatoes and corn on the cob are typical as sides, if you'll eat them."

"I'll eat just about anything," Melissa said with a laugh. "Especially when it comes from the land. Or sea," she added.

Stone grinned, then pushed back his chair. "Good. Then we're set. Want to eat here or at the cabin?"

"Does it matter to you?" Melissa asked him.

"Either place is just as easy. We just lay down a bunch of newspapers, eat on that, then clean up the heap at the end."

"Sounds like fun! I've never eaten fresh crab like that before," Melissa told him.

"Then you're in for a treat!" Stone said, standing. He cleared his plate and picked up hers. Melissa stared up at him as the numbers finally sank in.

"Did you say two *dozen* crabs?"

"They go quicker than you think. And what we don't eat tonight will make for a mighty fine crab dip later."

Stone helped Melissa in the kitchen, then headed back to his cabin to shave and dress for work. As he kissed her good-bye, Melissa couldn't help but think again how domestic her relationship with Stone already felt. It was as if the two of them had slipped into something they'd already learned how to do. Like how someone can pick up riding a bicycle after not having ridden one for decades—or how special long-term friends can reunite after a prolonged period of separation, yet reconnect as if no time has gone by at all.

With the Victrola put away, Melissa was able to clear her thoughts of Fiona and concentrate on work. She sat at the piano, a deep sense of peace washing over her. Somehow she sensed that everything would be all right, and that Homecoming Cove was a *good* place to be, somewhere she'd always been destined to visit. Already, her spirits were lighter and her productivity had skyrocketed. Meeting handsome, gray-eyed Stone had certainly played a part in her improved perspective, as well.

Stone was so kind and caring toward her. Before she could even say anything, it was like he anticipated her needs. That's exactly what had happened last night, when he'd been able to tell Melissa didn't want to be alone, but he'd also understood he shouldn't press her for anything more. Melissa had never met a man like Stone, and he intrigued her in so many ways. He had a colorful history and ambition for the future, probably a lot more ambition than most folks might guess. Melissa was glad he'd shared his hopes for the museum with her, and had no doubt that when Stone was ready, he'd make his dream a reality. Melissa was used to people who talked big but actually did very little. Stone was just the opposite. And when he took her in his arms, she felt transported to the moon. Melissa sighed out loud, missing Stone's company already. The best way to stop thinking about him was to put her mind on her work.

She opened the keyboard cover and slid it back, just as something loud creaked in the yard. Melissa slowly pivoted around on the piano bench to see the garden gate had flung itself ajar. There was obviously a logical explanation for that too, Melissa told herself. The wind was strong blowing off the cove, and the gate's latch was probably old. She'd mention it to Stone this evening and surely he'd be able to fix it. Now, she thought, turning back around and gently laying her hands on the ivories, it was time to play.

Chapter Twenty-Five

A few hours later, Melissa stopped working and stretched her arms over her head, lacing her fingers together and pushing them toward the ceiling to unkink them. She couldn't believe it: she was actually done! In just a handful of days, she'd finished the project that had plagued her for weeks in New York. Confidence surged through her. It felt great to be back in the game and no longer question her abilities. Now she saw she'd been wrong to think a mere relationship's turning sour could sabotage her talents. It would take far more than that. For music was in her; it was part of who Melissa was, in her soul.

Melissa heard a loud creak behind her and turned to stare out the window. The garden gate was swinging lazily back and forth in the breeze. She'd go shut it and take a look at the garden. She was due for a break anyhow. Melissa slipped into her heavy sweater and headed out the screened porch door. Crossing the patio, she strode toward the garden, which was positioned against one side of the barn. As she approached it, the gate swung forward. But before she could grab it, it slammed back in the opposite direction, opening a path into the garden. Melissa stepped onto the old brick walkway that had once been a pleasant path through rows of rosebushes. Now, weeds poked through the bricks, several of which were cracked and in need of replacement.

She laid her hand on the gate behind her to close it, but it slammed shut with a click. Tingles raced up her arm, and Melissa jerked back her hand, which suddenly felt icy cold. She looked up beyond the top of the gate and toward the house. Fiona's piano was perfectly centered in the parlor window. For an instant, Melissa thought she heard a faint hint of sound, a few chords of a sonatina. Then she realized she must be imagining it. Winds blustered about her, riffling her hair as the late-morning sun warmed her face. She tried to turn away, but was spellbound, her gaze locked on the window. The words she'd spoken to Stone came back to her: *music is the key.* There was something about Fiona's music, something that Melissa didn't understand but was meant to know. All artists expressed emotion through their work, and musicians were no different. What had Fiona been trying to say through her songs? Was it possible she was still trying to communicate something to Melissa—and Stone?

Melissa pulled her eyes away from the house and turned toward the garden, where dilapidated rosebushes sat on either side of the old brick walk. They had probably once been a gorgeous sight to behold: roses of all varieties and colors blooming beautifully before a white picket fence, against the backdrop of Homecoming Cove. Now, nothing remained but weathered old bushes punctuated by prickly dried thorns.

Melissa traversed the garden, taking first one route and then another around the well-organized space. A vertical structure stood at the rear of the garden opposite the entry gate and parlor window, abutting the barn. It was roughly five feet tall and four feet wide and composed mainly of brick. Near its center sat a defunct fountain set in a stone basin. The outer edges of the basin's backsplash were adorned with delicately painted rosebud-patterned tiles. Melissa noted the bricks framing the basin and its tile surround were likely once painted white to match the house and barn, because small flecks of that color remained in their pastel palette, which had turned a dusty rose over time. These bricks looked to be in the same rough condition as those on the walk. Many appeared loose and a few had even tumbled out of the structure completely, leaving small rectangular gaps in what had probably once been a lovely garden focal point.

Melissa slowly approached the empty fountain, wondering how long it had been since water had gurgled from the spigot at its base, sending a plume of spray rising high before descending into the bowl all around it. Melissa traced the path of where the water must have gone after passing through the fountain and was impressed to find small spouts opening at the base at either side of the structure. These led into narrow canals that passed nearly invisibly along the outer edges of the garden's brick path. It was an irrigation system! How clever! This fountain hadn't just been ornamental—it had been functional. Melissa found herself impressed, and wondering whether that had been Fiona's father's idea when he'd had this place built. Or perhaps Fiona herself had come up with it later, when she'd had the garden installed. In any case, it was a fascinating part to this property that was easy to miss. Melissa couldn't wait to tell Stone about it, and see if he already knew.

Melissa angled back toward the house, her gaze once again landing on Fiona's piano, and a heaviness settled in her heart. What an incredible place this must have been in its heyday. And what a lovely honeymoon house it would have made for Fiona and Lewis. Melissa remembered Stone's comment about maybe buying the house himself someday, and she wondered whether he really would. She wasn't sure what a property like this sold for, but with its historic home, the barn, the cabin, and fifty acres of land, it had to be worth a fortune, particularly given its waterfront location. It seemed hard to believe someone who lived as simply as Stone could have that kind of money. Yet it was a nice goal for him to strive toward. If Stone were to actually start his museum, perhaps one day he'd eventually amass the means to live here, not in the cabin as a caretaker, but as lord and master of the manor. Melissa's eyes panned the grand old house and she had a sweeping vision of her and Stone running the place together. Of him fishing off the dock and her tending blooming bushes in the garden. They could restore everything to its former glory, the two of them together.

Though she was all alone, Melissa felt herself blush at the ridiculous fantasy, her cheeks heating furiously at the notion of her and Stone living here together as man and wife. She relived the feel of Stone's lips pressed to her neck and prickles of anticipation raced through her. What would that be like, to actually be Stone's wife and have him make love to her completely, without holding back? Melissa released a deep sigh, realizing that would be wonderful. It didn't take much imagination to guess Stone would make an amazing lover. He was attentive and kind, and when his soulful gray eyes met Melissa's, her heart skipped a beat. And when he kissed her...Melissa was lost in his world, totally his, body and soul. Melissa sighed again, and recalled herself to the present.

She wanted to spend the evening with Stone without having to think about work. With a little more effort, she could finish up her project notes, the last thing that needed doing, before he got back at six o'clock. Now that she'd stretched her mind a bit by dreaming up those fantasies, Melissa needed to stretch her legs. She'd go for a brisk walk around the property, then make herself some lunch. What a wonderful break she'd enjoyed at Homecoming Cove. If only there was a way to make her time here last forever.

Chapter Twenty-Six

Stone picked up the potatoes and some freshly harvested corn from a produce stand, then placed his order for the crabs at the local fish market, agreeing to return to retrieve them one hour later. He used the interval to pay a social call on Captain Bill. Stone found his grandpa sitting on the back porch of his modest house, smoking his pipe and reading the newspaper. Bill looked up as Stone walked onto the porch from the kitchen.

"Wasn't expecting you this evening," he said.

Stone sat in a nearby chair and said mildly, "Guess that makes two of us who have surprised each other today."

Bill perched his pipe on the lip of an ashtray and folded his paper. "If you want to settle things sooner rather than later, that's okay by me." He squared his jaw and stared at Stone, waiting for his grandson to offer some explanation. But Stone didn't feel like explaining.

"What I'd like is for you to apologize."

Bill's bushy eyebrows shot up. "Apologize? For what?"

"For assuming the worst...and embarrassing Melissa."

"Well now, if she's embarrassed, I can hardly see how that's my fault. I'm not the one who was half naked in your arms."

Stone blew out a hard breath. "In case you haven't noticed, Melissa is over the age of eighteen. For that matter, so am I. Way over."

"That doesn't change facts." Bill leaned forward. "She's still a renter on the property. The property where you're employed."

"Nothing is like you think it is," Stone answered.

"What's that supposed to mean?"

"Melissa. She's..." Stone paused and ran a hand through his hair. "She's different. Special. I could see that right away."

"Next thing I know you'll be telling me Melissa thinks you're special too." Bill huffed. "Boy, this thing isn't right. Whatever it is that's going on between you has got to stop."

Stone pursed his lips before answering. "No."

Bill sighed and slowly shook his head. After a moment, he said, "All right. Then tell me. What do you plan to do once she's gone? Sit around moping like you did when Cathy—?"

"Captain—"

"It's Grandpa to you."

"Doesn't matter who you are. You don't have the right to run my affairs."

"I certainly have the right to care. She's a city girl, Stone. A polished gem from New York City. You, by contrast, are a rough-cut—"

"Virginia gentleman," Stone quickly asserted.

Bill laughed and picked up his pipe. "Is that what they call it these days?"

"Melissa would attest to that." Stone stood heatedly. "Not that it's any of your business. Not that any of this is!" He stormed for the kitchen door.

"Stone, wait!"

Stone turned partway on the threshold. Bill's eyes were weighted with sadness and his cheeks sagged. "You hardly know the girl. Is it really that serious?"

Stone answered hoarsely, "I think it could be."

"Then what about when she goes?" Bill asked softly. "What about when it's over?"

Stone gripped the doorframe and turned his head.

"Last time you left town. For ten *years*. Not just a few months. For a long time."

Stone met his eyes and Bill continued, his voice quaking. "I'm an old man, boy. I may not have another ten years in me."

Chapter Twenty-Seven

Melissa pulled open the door before Stone had a chance to knock. She'd heard his truck on the drive and raced downstairs to greet him. After a long walk in the country, she'd returned to finish her work, then decided to freshen up. She'd showered and changed into a new pair of jeans, boots, and a nice sweater. Melissa had even taken time to carefully style her hair and apply fresh makeup. She was practically decked out for an evening on the town. Only she was here in Homecoming Cove and not in some huge city. Melissa suddenly felt self-conscious, like she'd way overdone it. Would Stone think she was trying too hard?

He erased any doubts with a broad smile. "Wow!" he said, clutching a cardboard box with a couple of paper bags balanced on top of it. "You look terrific."

Melissa grinned at the compliment. "Thanks, Stone!" The fact was, he always looked dynamite to her, but she stopped herself from saying so. "Come on in."

He walked to the kitchen and set his box down on the center island while she closed the door behind him. "Anything else in the truck?" she asked as an afterthought.

"Not that we'll be needing now." Stone removed the paper bags and extracted a wine bottle from one of them. "The usual pairing is beer," he said, indicating the crabs. The warm scent of freshly steamed seafood wafted toward her. "But I noticed you don't keep any in the fridge, so I figured you for a wine person."

"You've got me figured out pretty well." Melissa laughed with delight and took the bottle from him, examining its label. "It's a Virginia wine," she said with mild surprise.

"And a very good one," he assured her. Stone removed his jacket and hung it on a hook by the door. "From the western part of the state."

"Shall we open it or wait for dinner?"

"Your call." Stone unfolded the top of the other bag and held it toward her. Melissa peered inside to find a few ears of corn and a small group of new potatoes.

"I'm so excited," Melissa said. "Dinner's going to be delicious."

"Speaking of which…" Stone said with a grin. "Mind if I get out some pots?"

"What can I do to help?" Melissa asked, all at once feeling helpless in her own house. Well, so okay, it wasn't really *her* house, but she felt so at home here it was easy to overlook that small detail.

"Why don't you grab some old newspapers from the stack by the recycle bin outside on the porch?" he suggested. "You can set up the table. Crab picks and mallets are in the drawer by the stove."

"You know this place pretty well," Melissa told him.

Stone shrugged and began shucking corn above the waste can. "I've mostly worked in the yard, but Captain

Bill occasionally asked me to assist him with minor repairs in here."

"Do you always call your granddad Captain Bill?"

Stone feigned consternation. "Not generally to his face."

Melissa laughed, understanding. "I tried calling my mom Laura once when I was in high school."

"I'm guessing from the *once* qualifier that didn't go over well," Stone said astutely.

"I was grounded for a week."

"Wow, your folks were tough."

"How about yours?" Melissa asked reflexively. Then she remembered. "Oh Stone, I'm sorry... I didn't mean to—"

"It's all right, Melissa. I don't mind talking about them." He dropped both ears of corn into a pot on the center island and dusted off his hands. "The truth is they were pretty tough too. But not tough in a bad way. All in all, they were pretty fair. Not that I gave them much to worry about." A sly smile crept up his lips. "I didn't really start getting into trouble until I moved up here."

"No way!" she cried in surprise. "You were the bad boy of Port Scarborough?"

"Something like that," he said obliquely.

"Bet that was fun for the captain."

"He took his duties seriously, I can tell you that. You don't know how many times I had to swab the deck!"

"The what?"

"That's what he called scrubbing the kitchen floor. Every time I got caught doing something I shouldn't have, I had to clean it—with a brush, and on my hands and knees." Melissa stifled a giggle trying to envision this. "I must say," Stone continued, "I think we had the most pristine kitchen floor on the entire peninsula. You could have eaten off of it!"

"Did the punishment work?" Melissa asked him. "Help keep you on the straight and narrow?"

"Not really," Stone answered honestly. "It did make me much more careful though…about not getting caught." He grinned again and Melissa suddenly wondered if he was exaggerating, or whether he'd really been that much trouble as a teenager.

"Well, you know what they say, don't you?"

He raised his head, waiting for her to continue.

"It's going to all come back at you, Stone," she said, teasing. "Someday when you have a child—"

"What if the mother is a saint?"

"Beg pardon?" Melissa asked, suddenly thrown.

Stone stopped what he was doing and took a step toward her. "The mother," he said. "My wife." Oddly, the word scraped from his throat. "Wouldn't she have some influence? I mean, genetically." Stone's gray gaze poured all over her and Melissa's face flushed hot.

"I…don't know. I mean, yes. I suppose—"

Stone dipped his chin toward hers and his voice was sultry. "Last time I checked, it took two to make a baby."

Melissa swallowed hard. Forget about her face, now her whole body felt on fire, consumed by big, lapping flames. "It does," she answered weakly. "It does take two." Not that Melissa had ever even considered having a baby until just now. Perhaps she'd thought about it abstractly on a few occasions. But she'd never envisioned it in specific terms. She'd never imagined producing a child with any certain man…until Stone. Melissa's heart leapt and her pulse raced at the very idea. All at once she knew Stone would make a wonderful father. Loving and playful, but stern when he needed to be.

"Are you a saint, Melissa?" Stone asked smoothly.

He met her eyes, and Melissa's skin tingled. "I'm hardly that."

Stone gently cupped her cheek with his hand. "I think it's better that way. Don't you? When both parents are normal people?"

Melissa was breathing so hard she could barely speak. "Normal is good," she said finally.

"I think normal's terrific," Stone answered huskily. Then he brought his mouth down on hers and kissed her. Melissa's knees threatened to give way so she clung to his shoulders. Then he brought his arms around her and pulled her in close, so her front was pressed to his rock-hard frame. Every inch of her body sizzled on contact. A tiny sound escaped her that was half-pant, half-purr, and Stone groaned in response, sliding his hands down her back as more of his anatomy came alive. Melissa molded herself against him, unable to resist his manly appeal. It made her want to be all woman—and totally his.

"You're going to make an awfully good mother," he growled between kisses.

"And you're going to make a really sexy dad," she eagerly returned.

Then both abruptly stopped and pulled apart. Stone stared down at Melissa and she stared back. Crimson streaked across his temples and colored the tops of his ears. His Adam's apple rose and fell. "I think..." he croaked hoarsely. "That we should make dinner."

Melissa blinked, her mind clearing as the tidal wave of passion began to ebb. She felt winded and out of sorts, like she'd nearly lost her mind for a moment. She'd practically been prepared to let Stone carry her up the stairs. Just a few more minutes in his arms—or one more hot kiss... *Yep, that would have done it,* Melissa thought, catching her breath. "Dinner's a great idea," she answered faintly.

Stone took a step back, as if coming out of a daze. "I'll finish cooking."

"And I'll get the newspaper."

"We should probably open the wine."

"To let it breathe," Melissa offered, thinking she could stand a little air too. Then she darted for the porch and stepped out into the evening, inhaling deeply. Oh yeah, she could imagine having babies with Stone. She could imagine it a little too clearly. *Whoa.* What was happening to her? Melissa quickly gathered up some newspapers and carted them back indoors, spreading them out on the dining room table. But as she laid down each page, her fingers trembled like shaking leaves. Stone Thomas would either be the end of her or offer up a brand new beginning. Melissa could see that now. There could be no in-between relationship with Stone. They were destined to be more than friends. But for how long? Melissa couldn't bear to contemplate the answer.

Chapter Twenty-Eight

A little while later, Melissa and Stone sat at the dining room table polishing off the wonderful Virginia wine Stone had brought. The table was cluttered with crab picks and mallets and in its center sat a mound of empty crab shells piled high. Stone set their two corn cobs on top of it and Melissa laughed. "That's quite a pile for the compost heap."

"I'll haul it out back in a few minutes," Stone told her. "No need letting good natural products go to waste."

"This wine is pretty tasty," Melissa said, licking her lips.

"Straight from the vine! Well…" Stone paused and smiled. "I suppose there's a bit of fermenting that goes on first."

Melissa laughed again, feeling contented. "I'm so glad I met you," she told him boldly. "And to think if I hadn't come out here—"

Stone reached over and took her hand. "But you did. That's what counts." His eyes met hers, questioning. "Isn't it?"

Melissa warmed in the heat of his stare. "Yes."

"What made you pick this house, by the way? What was it about Homecoming Cove?"

"I fell in love with the landscape," she admitted. "From the photos on the website, the place looked spectacular. It also seemed peaceful and far away, like someplace that would be perfect for composing. Plus," she added happily, "it was the only rental property I found that had a piano."

"How about that? Then I guess it was meant to be." Stone squeezed her hand, and Melissa believed the same thing in her heart.

"So! How did things go today?" Stone glanced around the dining room, then out the darkened window toward the barn. "Any more...disturbances?"

"No, everything went fine! I got a ton of work done. Really fabulous work too, if I say so myself," she said, preening just a little.

"Well, good for you!" It felt so great having the attention of a man like Stone, and he focused all his energy on her. "I was a little concerned about...well, you know." He released her hand and picked up his wine.

"Look, Stone, I don't know what happened with the Victrola, really I don't. But I do think some kind of vibration might have set it in motion."

"Vibration?"

"An earth tremor, something like that? Or maybe the crank is faulty. It could have stuck temporarily, then unwound itself and starting playing later."

"Melissa, that's impossible." Stone frowned into his wine, looking thoughtful a moment. "There's something I didn't tell you. When I was up in the attic this morning, it was like... Well, I'm not sure what. But I got a strange feeling."

She leaned toward him. "A feeling, Stone?"

He met her gaze with a serious expression. "A feeling that you're not safe here. That's what I was trying to tell you at breakfast."

"That's ridiculous."

"I know it sounds weird, but—"

"I've never felt more at home anywhere in my life!" Melissa burst in, realizing when she said it that the words rang true. There was something about Homecoming Cove that calmed her and made her feel settled. "I love being in this house. Especially…" Her throat felt raw as she whispered, "…with you."

"You don't know how much I love having you here," he said gently. "And how much I want you to stay, but if there's any chance—any chance at all that something might—"

"Stone, listen to me." Melissa set down her glass and the newspaper beneath it crinkled. "Nothing bad is going to happen, okay? Just look at us here tonight." Melissa's heart raced. "What I see looks pretty wonderful."

"The view's pretty fantastic from here too," Stone agreed.

"Then it's settled," Melissa told him. "Let's not worry anymore about eerie happenings that probably all have logical explanations anyway. Let's focus on the here and now."

Stone studied her face and his gray eyes glistened. "And what about tomorrow?"

Melissa hung her head. "I…don't know." And she didn't, she really didn't. What could she say? *I want to stay here forever. With you, Stone, with you.* Just because those thoughts pounded through her heart didn't mean they had any business working their way up to her head, much less out of her mouth. She had a life and career in New York, and Stone's future was clearly here. Hadn't he as much as told her so in admitting his ambition for founding the museum? When she looked up, she said, "It may not be my place to ask, and if you don't want to tell me, that's okay."

"Melissa," he said, taking her hand again. "I'm happy telling you everything. Anything you want to know."

"I was just wondering," she began cautiously. "About your time in the Caribbean. You were there a long while, and then suddenly came home. It made me think that maybe you had an involvement…"

He watched her patiently, waiting.

Melissa inhaled sharply, then spilled it. "A woman, Stone," she said quickly. "I guess I'm asking if there was anyone serious. I mean, you're a nice-looking man, and…" Stone smiled warmly and she stopped talking.

"There was someone, yes. A long time ago. But not in the Caribbean; right here, locally."

"What happened?"

Stone tightened his grip around her fingers. "I suppose she wanted greater adventure than she thought I could offer. We were pretty steady—or so I thought— for our last two years of high school. We talked about things the way high-school kids do…the future…maybe even having a family together someday. It seemed like a heady fantasy, something very far off, but fun to think about. At the time, I was only eighteen and way too young to think about settling down."

"But this girl…?"

"Cathy."

"She had other plans?" Melissa inquired gently.

"Apparently so." Stone laughed bitterly. "A week before high-school graduation, she broke up with me by telling me she was marrying Johnny. Johnny was a mutual friend," Stone explained. "He and I weren't super close, but he was in the group that Cathy and I hung with."

"Why Johnny?"

"He'd enlisted in the Marines and was deploying shortly. I suppose he offered Cathy the type of life she wanted...and the chance to get out of Port Scarborough."

"Have you heard from her?"

"Not directly, but through the grapevine. Some other guys who were in our group keep up with Johnny. He and Cathy are still together and apparently happy. They've got three kids and a mortgage now."

"I'm sorry, Stone. That must have been hard." She surveyed the lines of his face, which were etched deep by the painful memory. "Is that why you left town?"

"I left for a lot of reasons. But that was part of it, yeah. There was a certain humiliation to being ditched in front of my group of friends. Plus, despite what Cathy thought, I did want to get out and see the world. But, more important..." He met her eyes. "I wanted to discover myself."

"And did you do that?" she asked softly.

Stone swallowed hard and answered, "Yeah, I think that I did." He finished the rest of his wine, then turned the conversation around to her. "You never really told me about Peter."

Melissa sighed deeply. "There's really not much to tell, other than the fact that he was a jerk. Thought himself way better than me."

"It's hard to see how anyone could do that."

"Well, he did. And he told me…" Her chin quivered slightly. "Said at one point that I wasn't the type of girl guys like him marry."

"*What?*" Stone exploded angrily, before reining himself in. "Then the guy was an idiot. First for thinking that and second for saying it. What kind of a man was he, anyway? What made him think he was so special?"

"He came from money," Melissa replied sadly. "Big money and the country club set. If you didn't golf or play tennis, you obviously weren't worth dealing with."

"But he dated you."

"I didn't realize he viewed me as transitional," she said, the hurt apparent in her voice.

Stone reached toward her and cupped her chin in his hand. "Anyone who would view you that way is a fool, Melissa. I hope that you know that."

She smiled wanly, his touch still grazing her skin. "*Like attracts like,* Peter said. *That's how it's meant for the long haul.*"

"I can't believe that's always true," Stone said, his face drawing near. "Oftentimes opposites attract."

Stone's hand slid to her cheek, then around to the nape of her neck. Melissa's breathing quickened. "Are we opposites, Stone?"

"I think we're alike in some very important ways."

His mouth drew nearer and Melissa sighed. "Such as?"

"Such as…" Stone brushed his lips over hers. "We both value kindness…" He kissed her again. "And honesty…"

"And history…" she murmured as his lips claimed hers a third time.

An urgent squeak came from the yard and they broke apart, staring out the dining room window. The white garden gate sat wide open.

"I meant to tell you," Melissa said. "It's been doing that all day. I think the catch must have come loose."

"I'll take a look at it tomorrow," Stone assured her. "Likely an easy fix, and I'd hate for it to keep bothering you while you're here."

"Thank you," Melissa said, standing. "Meanwhile, we should probably clean up." Stone got to his feet as well. He set aside the crab utensils, then began balling up the newspaper with the trash inside it.

Stone glanced back out the window, then said hoarsely, "I think I should probably stay here tonight."

"What? No!" Melissa instantly regretted her vehement reaction.

"I meant in one of the guestrooms, Melissa."

"It's not…that," she stammered, thinking that partway it was. She was still sorting so much out in her head, including how she felt about Stone and what that might mean for her future. "It's just that I'm really fine. Fine to be here by myself. I think you should go on back to your cabin."

He eyed her doubtfully. "I don't see what it would hurt if I—"

"What if Captain Bill drops by?" she interjected quickly.

"What? In the middle of the night?"

"He seems to appear first thing in the morning."

"That's true, and I'm sorry. I talked to him about that."

"Oh, Stone. Did you really? I'm so embarrassed by what he must have thought."

"Don't worry," Stone said. "He'll come around."
Then he grumbled under his breath, but Melissa still
heard it: "Hopefully, come around to apologize." Stone
arranged the bunched-up newspapers in a wad and went
to grab his jacket, while Melissa carried the rest of the
things into the kitchen. He met her in the hall on his
way outdoors. "Okay," Stone relented. "If that's the
way you really want it, I won't stay here tonight. I'll go.
But do you think I could stay a little while longer first?"
His gray gaze poured all over her and Melissa's cheeks
steamed.

"I'd like that," she said, smiling sweetly. "I'd like
that very much."

"Good," Stone answered. "Then while I'm out
back, I'll grab some fresh logs for the fire. I can build
us one in the living room and we can enjoy another
bottle of that Virginia wine you liked so much."

"Another bottle?" Melissa asked.

Stone surprised her with a grin. "Brought a backup
bottle in my truck."

They spent a wonderful couple of hours gathered in
each other's arms and sipping their wine. Flames leapt
in the fireplace before them, warming their faces and
their toes. Stone had kicked off his shoes and Melissa
had removed her boots when they'd settled in beneath
the fuzzy throw blanket that now covered them both. It
was just like living in a dream, Melissa thought, as the
first flecks of snow started to fall outside. "I didn't
expect winter weather down here in October," she said,
snuggling up against him.

Stone held her close. "We get some, but nothing
like you do up north. Compared to New York, the
season's balmy."

Melissa laughed contentedly. "Probably so."

Stone kissed the top of her head and glanced toward the fire. "This is really nice."

"Mmm," Melissa agreed, her heart soaring. Being with Stone felt natural. He was so tender and warm, yet strong in his own way. And when his arms were around her, it was like the rest of the world melted away.

Stone nibbled the top of her ear, then gave a husky whisper. "I wish I didn't have to go."

Melissa giggled and hugged him to her, wrapping her arms around his neck. "Yeah, but you do, you know."

He shifted her in his embrace so he could view her fully, his face angled down toward hers. "Of course," he said, smiling sexily. "But don't make me go just yet."

Melissa's pulse pounded and her temperature spiked. "Stone…"

His chin dipped toward hers. "Hmm?"

"Okay," she relented in a breathy whisper. "Not just yet."

And then he kissed her very deeply for a long, luxurious time.

Chapter Twenty-Nine

Stone slept in fits and starts. Each time he relaxed, the dream closed in through the darkness, that thin chain dangling just out of reach in the murky depths. But this time, as he stretched toward it in the water, something more came into view: Fiona's heart-shaped locket and the cuff of a sleeve. Stone recognized it as the sleeve of an old sea captain's jacket, like the one his great-great uncle Lewis might have worn. Yet Stone's arm extended from it, his hand desperately grabbing for that floating gold chain. Stone sat bolt upright, his chest heaving, and flipped on the light. His eyes gradually adjusted to its brightness as his gaze traveled the room. Finally, he found the memory box.

Stone pushed back the covers and strode toward the box with purpose. He hoisted it off the floor and carried it to the coffee table, where he quickly worked it open. Stone threw back the lid and fished in the bottom of the trunk with his fingers until he found the small hand-carved box holding Fiona's locket. He opened it, set the lid aside, and extracted the thin gold chain, dangling it from one hand. It glimmered in the lamplight as the locket twirled beneath it, suspended in the air. Stone's heart hammered harder as the realization hit him. It *had been* Fiona's locket in his dream all these years. But that wasn't all.

Stone thought back to the day his dad, David, had given him the memory box. It was shortly after David's mother and Stone's maternal grandmother, Jocelyn, had died. The box had belonged to Jocelyn, and Jocelyn's mother, Amelia, before her. Amelia had taken it into her possession from her mother, Mary, who'd been Lewis's sister. Captain Lewis Stone had been the original owner of the box.

Stone recalled feeling overwhelmed by the enormity of the gift. It seemed such a great treasure to bestow on such a young boy. And yet, he'd felt honored his dad had entrusted him with these sacred family heirlooms. Stone's dad routinely commented that Stone was a very capable boy, with the maturity of others twice his age. He'd given him the memory box shortly after his mother's passing, to prove just how much faith he inspired. *Your grandmother wanted you to have this,* David had said with a warm fatherly smile. When Stone had asked in his eight-year-old innocence what he was to do with it, his dad had confidently replied, *Someday you'll know.*

But Stone hadn't known...or completely understood. Until now. He lifted the locket higher, then lowered it into his other palm, closing his fingers around it. It wasn't just Stone's past that was caught up in this memory box; somehow it encapsulated his future. A future that went beyond starting the maritime museum and on to something more. "Why, Fiona? Why?" he asked aloud, more firmly grasping the locket. "Why was this so important to you?" Instinctively, Stone knew it had been, and this had something to do with it being in his dream.

While Stone had naturally assumed the locket had been special to his great-great uncle, Stone hadn't anticipated the locket's full significance until now. Stone recalled the sleeve of the sea captain's jacket from his latest dream and slapped his forehead with his free hand. Another truth became clear. It wasn't Stone who'd been drowning in his dreams all these years. It had been his great-great uncle, Lewis Stone.

Melissa awoke to a rush of cool air blasting into her room. She opened her eyes and warily studied the shadows. Something appeared to be moving in the hall. It couldn't possibly be Stone coming back to check on her? No, that hardly made sense. She'd locked all the doors when he'd gone…after kissing him good night for maybe the twentieth time. Melissa sighed under the covers, then felt a gust of wind against her cheek again. Slowly raising her head from the pillow, Melissa stared at the door while supporting herself on her elbows. It was partially ajar, opening inward from the hall. Then *wham*—a force crashed against it from the other side.

Melissa trembled under the comforter. Something was right outside her room. And that something had just slammed into the bedroom doorframe. She had two choices: she could either cower under the covers or confront whatever lurked in the hall. Melissa cast the bedclothes aside and placed her bare feet on the floor. When she stood, her knees shook and her legs felt rubbery. *It's better to go out and face it*, she told herself resolutely. *Besides, maybe it's only the wind.* Yes, but if that were the case, just where was it coming from? Melissa stood unsteadily, then rapidly gripped the bedpost when her knees threatened to give. *Thump!* Something banged against the far side of the door.

Melissa's heart rose in her throat as it sounded a second time and then a third. It was like a heavy thudding or knocking. Melissa tried to speak or cry out, but her mouth was sandpaper dry, her lips cracking with the effort.

Perhaps Stone had been right, she thought in a panic. Perhaps she should have gone. Or she should at least have let him stay the night. Now she was alone with... *Thump!* There it went again! Melissa's palms went slick and her stomach plummeted like an elevator cage that had been cut from its cables. All at once she feared she might throw up...or pass out... No! That would leave her helpless. And Melissa refused to be helpless. Refused to be a victim anymore. Not to Peter, nor to her own insecurities. She was strong, she was independent, and she was free to choose her own destiny. Free to fall in love with a loner with stunning gray eyes. Free to stay at Homecoming Cove, if that's what her heart desired. And nobody, not even a ghost, was going to stop her!

Summoning her courage, Melissa raced for the door, propelled by sheer determination. She reached for the doorknob, her heart pounding, and yanked back the door, greeting the blackness of the hall. That's when she saw that the door leading to the attic's staircase had blown open and had been banging into her doorframe and part of the adjoining wall in a draft that billowed back and forth from the top of the attic stairs. Perhaps air had been blowing in through the roof vents and creating a vacuum. Or perhaps it had been something more. Icy claws seemed to wrap around her, chilling her down to the bone in their steely grip. Melissa balled her hands into fists and yelled up the attic stairs. "I'm not afraid of you, Fiona! Do you hear me? Not afraid!"

she shouted, cursing herself when her voice warbled. Then, to Melissa's utter astonishment, the attic door in front of her slammed shut.

Chapter Thirty

Stone phoned Melissa the next morning to say he'd stop by after lunch to take a look at the garden gate. If it required repairs, he could pick up what he needed the following afternoon from the hardware store, then stop by after work to fix it. Since it was Sunday and the hardware store wasn't open today, Stone could have just as easily waited to check on the gate Monday morning. But he didn't want to wait an extra day to see her. Not when all he could think of was holding Melissa in his arms. Plus, he'd had a stunning revelation, and he burned to share it with her. Fiona's locket, and Lewis, and Stone's dreams—were all incredibly connected. The only thing Stone still didn't know was why the locket was so important.

Stone's primary mission now was ensuring Melissa's safety. When he'd called to ask if Melissa had had a good night's rest, she'd said something about insomnia and waking up early, then not being able to go back to sleep. Stone had experienced much the same thing, but for different reasons. He'd been analyzing the nature of his dream, and had decided it was figurative for the most part. Lewis had been symbolically trying to hold on to his dearest love, even as his own life faded. It was a troublesome event to relive again and again.

Stone had sat up long into the night pondering Lewis's fate and wondering how he, as a distant relative could have somehow accessed some of Lewis's memories.

Stone had heard of the controversial study of memory DNA, the notion that not only genetic markers get passed down from one generation to the next, but that also some of a human's fiercest emotional experiences might create genetic imprints of their own. If an ancestor had experienced a certain kind of tragedy—and if it were traumatic enough—perhaps that could cause alterations in the familial DNA that could also be inherited down the line. Whether it was memory DNA or somehow concocted out of Stone's boyhood imagination, one fact remained. Stone was now convinced his recurrent dream was more about Lewis than himself, and that it had to do with Lewis's remorse over losing Fiona. Stone had sensed that Fiona's spirit was unsettled. Was it possible that Lewis's soul was restless too? Had the two of them been trying to reach out to him and Melissa in some uncanny way? Fiona through her music, and Lewis via Stone's recurring dreams?

Stone didn't fully understand the reasons behind the disturbances at Homecoming Cove, but he still worried that Melissa might be in danger. He didn't feel right letting her stay alone in that house, and today he would tell her so and insist on one of two things. If Melissa was determined to stay on the property to fulfill the course of her short-term lease, she could either stay in the cabin with Stone, or he'd move into the big house with her. Stone didn't care about what his grandfather thought, or how things might appear to the townspeople.

In his heart of hearts, Stone honestly wasn't ready for Melissa to return to New York. They were building something together. Something phenomenal. Stone felt this in his soul. Yet if there were any more hints of danger around Melissa, Stone was prepared to stay strong and convince her to leave. Not forever, just until Stone believed it was safe for Melissa to return. Stone had always loved the House at Homecoming Cove, and for quite some time had yearned to own it. He still wished to make it his and live there someday. *Hopefully with a wife and kids,* he found himself thinking. Stone's heart beat harder as he realized what he really wanted. He wanted that wife to be Melissa, and those children to be theirs.

Chapter Thirty-One

When Stone arrived at the house later, he found Melissa huddled up in a sweater drinking coffee on the screened porch, with a blanket draped over her knees.

"Not too chilly for you?" Stone asked, coming in through the back door. The evening snowflakes had subsided, giving way to the first hard frost. Though it had coated the lawn at daybreak, by noontime the sun had cast its warming glow across the property and the day had heated up considerably.

"I could probably do with a hot kiss," she flirted, gazing up at him.

Stone grinned and planted one on her as she sat in the big wicker chair. Though she was still as beautiful as ever, Stone couldn't help but notice the dark circles beneath her eyes. "I'm sorry you had trouble sleeping."

"It's okay," Melissa answered a tad evasively. "I'm hoping things will be more settled now."

"What's that supposed to mean?"

She shrugged and studied his features. "You look a little ragged yourself. More bad dreams?"

"Yes, but no! I mean, Melissa," he said, with growing excitement, "just wait until you hear what I have to tell you."

"Will this take long?" she questioned.

"It might," Stone admitted, shoving his hands in his pockets. One of them held Fiona's locket and his fingertips grazed against it.

"Then let me get a refill," she said, lifting her cup. "Can I pour some for you?"

"I'd love it."

A little while later, Melissa sat there stunned, listening raptly to Stone's story. He passed her Fiona's locket and she took it in her hand. "You know, Stone, I think you're right. Your dream was much more about Lewis than you, in spite of what you said happened to you in the Caribbean. That must have been very scary for you, going overboard."

"Yeah, especially since it felt like it had all happened before."

"In a way it had. Way back in your past." She stopped and corrected herself. "Your family's past, anyway."

"I've never liked the water," he told her.

"You were a sailor!"

"I mean, I've been drawn to it, and enjoyed working on it. I just don't like being *in it,* as in swimming."

"Are you a strong swimmer?"

"Was the captain of my high-school swim team and earned my lifeguarding certificate."

"But why, if…?"

"I couldn't let it control me, Melissa. I had to take charge. Can you understand that?"

She glanced back into the house and was quiet a minute. "Yes," she eventually said. "I think that I can." She stared down at the locket in her palm. "I wish we knew more about this, and why it's so important.

Because I agree with you, I suspect that it is. Or at least that it *was* very important to Lewis at one time."

Stone checked his watch, seeing that nearly forty minutes had elapsed. He'd been so engaged with Melissa, he'd nearly forgotten he had an errand to run for his boss, Mac. A boat was docking in Port Scarborough that required a replacement outboard motor and Stone had offered to take care of the job, because he knew it could be done quickly. "I hate to do this to you, but I promised my boss I'd tackle a quick job in town this afternoon. Maybe we can finish our discussion this evening?"

She smiled softly. "I'd like that."

"I can bring pizza," Stone offered.

"You provided the food last night," she told him brightly. "I'll cook." She handed him back Fiona's locket and he slid it into his pocket.

"Let me take a quick look at that gate before I go. Could be I've got what I need at the shop. If not, I'll grab it from the hardware store tomorrow."

Stone's heart was light as they walked toward the garden. The sky was blue and big puffy clouds billowed overhead, casting shadows on the shimmering waters of the cove. This was an amazing place, somewhere Stone could see himself living for years. But in the big house, not in the caretaker's cabin. Stone recalled his first conversation with Melissa when he'd mentioned perhaps buying the property in the future. Of course, then he'd hardly known Melissa at all and had been speaking of buying the house for himself. Looking at her now in the midst of this beautiful day, Stone found himself longing to buy it for her. For the two of them, so they could live here together. Perhaps even, eventually, with children.

Stone wondered how Melissa would respond to the notion that he had incredibly entertained twice in one day. Would she be receptive, or recoil from him— feeling as if he were unnecessarily rushing their relationship along? If there was anything Stone didn't want to do, it was to push Melissa away. In his heart, he didn't want her to leave Homecoming Cove at all, unless it was out of fear for her safety. And hopefully, all those fears were now put aside. Since he'd returned the Victrola to the attic, things around the grounds appeared to have calmed down.

Stone approached the garden gate and pushed it open. Then he bent down on one knee to examine its latch. "It might have come a little loose," he said. "But it's a very minor repair. Nothing that a screwdriver can't fix."

"You can do that this evening?" Melissa asked.

"No need to wait. This will just take a minute. I've got tools in the barn."

Chapter Thirty-Two

While Stone disappeared to retrieve his tools, Melissa walked through the gate to once again trace the garden's footpath with measured steps. She spied the small rivulets on either side of the brick walk, remembering she'd wanted to mention the old irrigation system to Stone. He returned a few minutes later to find her standing by the base of the wall with its defunct fountain. "I was looking at this the other day," she said, glancing over her shoulder. "It's really fantastic. This must have been a spectacular garden once upon a time."

"I'm sure it was pretty with the fountain running," Stone said. He was already on his knees tightening the gate latch.

"Not just pretty," Melissa said. "Functional."

Stone quickly finished his work and stood. "What do you mean?"

"Look down." Melissa pointed to the outer edges of the brick path. "The run-off went down there...to water the roses."

"Ingenious." Stone met her eyes and smiled, and then his face went ashen. Melissa heard the crumbling sound behind her seconds before Stone called out her name. In a flash, Stone sprinted toward her, yanking her off her feet and out of the way of a tumbling tower of bricks that crashed to the ground and smashed apart on the walkway. Melissa's heart pounded in her throat.

"What happened?" she asked in a daze.

"You almost got hit!"

Melissa gaped at the rubble near their feet, then stared back at the dismantled fountain behind them. The plummeting bricks had burst apart as if exploding, and the lovely decorative tiles had been smashed to smithereens. Clouds of dust rose from the massive pile burying the cracked stone basin. Melissa felt the blood drain from her face. "Something must have…come loose," she said, feeling a chill run through her. "The bricks, they were old and—"

"No!" Stone took her in his arms and gave her an urgent look. "Melissa, listen to me. That was too close. You could have been hurt. Seriously hurt!"

"You can't tell me you think that was Fiona?" Melissa asked, reading the panic in his eyes.

Just then a cacophony of sound erupted from the house and both stared through the parlor window at the piano. Several discordant notes had just sounded together in a clash. "It was my notepad," Melissa explained breathlessly. "It must have fallen from the rack just when—"

"You mentioned Fiona's name?" Stone asked doubtfully.

"But why would she try to hurt me?" Melissa questioned. "What have I done?"

"Nothing," Stone continued in a gravelly tone, "other than make me fall in love with you."

He tightened his embrace. "Melissa, something's going on here, something that defies rational explanation. I want you in my life, I do. But not if it means putting you in danger."

"But I'm not in danger! I'm not!" Even as she said it, her chin trembled.

Stone searched her eyes. "Melissa, what are you not telling me?"

"Last night," she said faintly. "There was a noise—probably the wind—coming from the attic."

"It woke you?" Stone asked with concern.

"It slammed shut the attic door."

Stone set his chin. "That does it, you're not staying."

"But Stone, I—"

"I don't know what's going on, but until it's settled—until everything's settled—you're better off in New York than here."

Melissa stared at him pleadingly. "I'm better off with you."

"And I with you." He kissed her firmly. "But I don't want you to stay. Not now."

"But you can't..." Her voice broke apart. "Can't just push me away. I'm paying to stay here."

"I'll see that you get your money back. All of it."

"It's not about the money, Stone." She gazed up at him and tears blurred his image.

"Hey." He drew her up against him and gently kissed her forehead. "Everything will be okay. We'll be okay. You'll see."

Melissa was at war with herself. Part of her believed Stone was right, and that she'd be out of her mind to stay here. But another more stubborn part said that Stone was wrong. That she wasn't truly in danger. Neither of them was. She glanced back through the parlor window at the piano, still sensing music was the key. Music and Fiona...and this place...and Lewis... Somehow they all came together in a compelling way that needed unlocking. Melissa just didn't know how to achieve that. Apparently, neither did Stone, and now he was driving her away, insisting she go back to New York. But for her own safety. Because he cared. More than cared. It dawned on Melissa like a harmonic blast. Stone had just said he loved her. "You…you love me?" she asked, her lips quivering.

"Yes." He gave her a feathery light kiss. "I do. I can't help it Melissa, but I'm a goner. Totally yours."

She looked up at him as tears streamed down her cheeks. "That's pretty amazing," she said. "Because I've fallen in love with you too."

"Then let's not waste those emotions," Stone said surely. "Let's protect them. Pack your bags and go back to New York. I'll come for you."

"When?"

Stone hung his head.

"You don't know, do you?" she challenged. "There's no time frame on this. It could go on forever." Then another thought occurred. "Or…it could completely stop the moment I'm gone."

"It might," he said, meeting her eyes.

"Stone," she told him fiercely. "I don't want to run from this place, I don't want to let Fiona push me out."

"One week. Just one week, Melissa," he told her. "Just take that time away and I'll figure something out."

"And if you don't?"

"At least I'll know you'll be safe."

"This is ridiculous, Stone."

"Then humor me," he said with a desperate expression. "Please."

Melissa didn't want to leave, but she couldn't see how she could continue to protest. All her arguments had been laid out and rebutted. While she didn't want to believe she was in danger, she had been badly shaken by the episode with the attic door. The Victrola playing by itself had also been a little eerie. And what about her late-night walk down the dock, and this more recent event with the tumbling brick wall? There was the garden gate that continually swung open and… Melissa's gaze trailed back to the house and the parlor window. The piano.

Everything centered back on the piano. From this perspective, it was framed by the garden gate and sat exactly opposite the high brick wall that had held the fountain. She'd heard it playing by itself more than once, and Stone had heard it too. Even if she was imagining things, it was unlikely that she and Stone would share that joint lunacy. Though Melissa still wasn't one hundred percent convinced Fiona was a threat to her, neither could she prove that something wasn't. Something—or someone—had been causing disturbances at Homecoming Cove, and those disturbances had turned very dangerous indeed. If Stone hadn't been there to save her, and Melissa had become trapped under the debris from that falling wall, she wasn't sure what might have happened to her. "Okay," she finally agreed. "I'll go. But one week, Stone. One week," she said, weeping and despising her own weakness. "Then I'll expect you to call me."

Chapter Thirty-Three

Stone waited outside on the porch for Melissa to pack her things, planning to accompany her when she exited the property. He'd phoned Mac to see if someone else could install the motor, and Mac said his son Paul could do it, no problem. Mac didn't question what was wrong, but he could sense the urgency in Stone's voice. Stone frequently volunteered and rarely asked for favors, so when he'd called with a change of plans, Mac had been happy to oblige. Stone didn't know what was going on with the House at Homecoming Cove, but he was done with taking chances. Too many mishaps had occurred since Melissa's arrival. While certain events, like the attic vent covering coming loose and the gate latch not seating properly, might be attributed to the age of the place, other things had been blatantly spooky, like that old Victrola playing by itself and Stone hearing piano music in the middle of the night—all the way from over at the cabin. The garden wall may have been about to crumble anyhow, but the fact that it had collapsed in a heap while Melissa had been standing directly in front of it had been downright scary.

If amenities around the property were in such poor condition, then renters had no business staying here. But Stone had an inkling that the recent spooky happenings had far more to do with Melissa than the age and state of the property. If she wasn't the trigger, then why hadn't Stone witnessed or heard anything that seemed amiss before? Yes, he'd heard tales of fishermen anchored in the cove hearing piano music, but he had never given those stories much credence. They seemed like local lore that had taken on a life of its own, growing larger and more fantastic over time.

Have you heard about the House at Homecoming Cove? someone would say. *The property won't sell because it's haunted. A famous pianist died there of a broken heart, and she can still be heard playing her piano there today...* Stone had heard rumors of the mysterious piano playing at Homecoming Cove since he was in high school. He'd been with a group of teens who'd dared each other to row into the cove one cloudy Halloween evening, all in anticipation of meeting a ghost. Yet Stone hadn't heard anything. He frankly never believed anyone really had—until Melissa's arrival, when he'd first heard the piano music himself.

Stone fingered the locket in his pocket, thinking of Fiona. If her spirit did in fact still walk these grounds, what had made her so terribly restless now? Could it be that Melissa also being a musician had touched a chord with the original owner of the house? Had Melissa's playing the piano reawakened Fiona's spirit—and sparked some kind of spiritual connection between Melissa and Fiona? Or were things even more dire than that, and did Fiona envy Melissa for stealing the heart of the last remaining Lewis Stone heir, while Fiona's true love was lost to her forever? There were too many questions and not enough answers. Until he found a way to learn more, Stone feared Melissa wasn't safe at Homecoming Cove. Though his heart wrenched at the thought, he was glad she was leaving. But Stone wanted her to return, and he ached to own this property: all fifty acres, including the outbuildings and this house—and share them with Melissa.

Stone stared out at the water and the seagulls sailing above it. This was meant to be *his* place, *his* home. He'd sensed that ever since his return from the Caribbean. When the groundskeeper position came open, he'd asked his grandfather to put in a good word for him. Far beyond just caring for the lawn, Stone yearned to live on the land. The moment he'd moved into the cabin, Stone had felt at home. He was centered and at peace, slowly putting together his plan for the mariner's museum. The longer he lived on the grounds, the more Stone could see the House at Homecoming Cove eventually becoming his.

Then, when he'd begun falling for Melissa, Stone had developed a new vision for the property. He imagined bringing it back as a working farm, growing wheat and corn, and lovingly restoring the rose garden. Melissa would have a serene environment in which to compose her music, and Stone could busy himself with running things here and starting up the museum. One day, there might even be children scampering about, chasing each other across the manicured lawn and fishing from the dock. It was an idyllic dream. Stone's fingers tightened around the locket and released it. And now, some phantom had threatened it. Stone didn't know how, but he intended to get to the bottom of things at Homecoming Cove. He had to devise a way to set things right, so Melissa could come back here to live. Hope bloomed in Stone's heart. Perhaps even as his wife.

Chapter Thirty-Four

Twenty minutes later, Stone held Melissa in his arms and kissed her good-bye. He'd helped her load the SUV after assisting her with packing up the items from the kitchen, including things from the freezer and refrigerator that went in a large cooler. Melissa didn't want to go, but the truth was that her work here was done. She'd completed her project early, and had only hoped to spend more time with Stone. Now, he was promising they would share even more time together *in the future.* As he'd said those words, a quiet promise had emanated from his smoky gray eyes. Melissa wrapped her arms around his neck and hugged him to her. "I'm going to miss you," she whispered.

Stone squeezed her tightly and kissed the top of her head. "And I'll miss you."

He smelled musky and manly, like the clean scent of soap spiked with exotic spice. Cool autumn winds blew, bowing the limbs of the trees. "Say good-bye to Captain Bill for me." Melissa's cheek was still pressed to Stone's shoulder. He reached up to stroke her hair.

"I will."

"And tell him…" She pushed back in his embrace to meet his eyes. "Everything's not as it seemed."

"No," Stone said solemnly. "It's much, much more."

He gazed deeply into her eyes and Melissa's heart fluttered.

"Melissa." Stone gently cupped her face in his palms. "Say you'll come back to me."

The wind picked up, sending red and gold leaves twirling beneath the bright blue sky.

"I'll come back," Melissa whispered hoarsely.

Stone gave her a slow, sexy smile and covered her mouth with a kiss. She sighed into him then, wishing she could always stay in his arms, yet knowing she had to move on. At least for today. Tomorrow was another story. Her heartbeat quickened, then pounded harder, as Melissa anticipated what tomorrow might hold. In a way, she couldn't imagine leaving New York. But in another more urgent sense, every inch of her being longed to remain here. With Stone. At Homecoming Cove.

Stone spoke huskily between tender kisses. "I'll wait for you."

Melissa climbed behind the wheel of her SUV, feeling heat burn in her eyes. She willed herself not to cry and to be strong. This time at the Virginia Eastern Shore had delivered so much more than she'd hoped for. She'd not only accomplished her professional objectives, she'd also become more in tune with herself. Plus, she'd met an incredible man she probably would not have known otherwise. Stone was sexy, and caring, and oh so wonderful to her in so many ways. She could foresee building a relationship with him on a solid foundation: their mutual trust and respect for one another. And how he took her breath away when he kissed her… If they'd become even more intimate than that, Melissa wasn't sure if she could have pulled herself away. Thank goodness Stone had also had the good sense to forestall a full-fledged physical relationship. Melissa recalled Stone's words in the cabin, when he'd said if he made love to her, he'd never be able to let her go, and her skin tingled. She'd never want him to let go, either. Melissa already felt that way. It didn't take going to bed with Stone to know. And someday, when they finally did give themselves to each other fully, Melissa had no doubt it would be fantastic. Stone was so commanding and self-assured, yet equally loving and tender. How could he be anything but an amazing lover?

Melissa glanced in her rearview mirror, spotting Stone's truck closing in behind her. He caught her gaze on his windshield and gave her a mock captain's salute. Melissa giggled, recalling the first time he'd done that, and how the gesture had made her heart skip a beat. Just look at her now. Melissa had given Stone her heart completely. She'd said she loved him, and he'd said he loved her. It was hard to believe their emotions had deepened to that point in this amount of time. But in another way, it was as if the two of them had known each other forever.

Melissa centered her eyes back on the winding driveway ahead of her just in time to spy a huge dark object hurtling toward her SUV. It was an enormous oak tree! It slammed toward her with force, as if it had been felled at its base. Wavering outstretched limbs frantically combated the wind, as the monstrosity careened toward Melissa's windshield. She shrieked and punched her brake pedal to the floor.

Melissa's SUV screeched to a halt, her heart hammering against her rib cage. Stone stopped abruptly behind her, his truck's tires grating loudly against gravel, his vehicle barely avoiding a collision with hers. The tree thundered to the ground, just grazing Melissa's front bumper. Melissa fell forward, gripping the steering wheel, blood pounding in her ears. Lifeless brown leaves attached to spindly twigs and branches plastered themselves against her windshield. Through their spiderweb pattern, she could spy the gigantic trunk of the tree that now lay sideways across the driveway, blocking her escape.

A door popped open and Stone clambered out of his truck, racing to her driver's side window. "Melissa!" he called frantically. "Are you all right?"

She sat back in her seat and brought her hands to her head, unable to believe what had just happened. She'd nearly been killed! Just a few feet farther and... Bile rose in her throat. Stone was right. He'd been so right. It was dangerous here. He reached for her door handle and yanked it open, leaning into the cab and placing his hands on her shoulders. "Sweetheart," his said, his breath ragged. "Look at me."

Melissa slowly turned to face him.

Stone's eyes were wide with worry. "Are you hurt?"

Melissa numbly shook her head, then Stone stepped back to survey the damage. "There will be no getting you out of here without a chainsaw," he said. "Fortunately, I keep one in the barn." Stone stood alert, then spun toward the house. His countenance stiffened. "What's that?"

Melissa followed Stone's line of vision to the old farmhouse. She'd packed in such a hurry, she'd forgotten to close one of the front windows she'd cracked to let in fresh air. It was the front window to the parlor. A violent torrent of piano music pealed through it. Melissa's palms went slick and slipped off the steering wheel. Stone turned back to her and glanced at the fallen oak, his expression dark. Then he grated, "Fiona."

Melissa unhitched her seatbelt and stumbled from the SUV, her legs unsteady. Stone extended his hand and she took it, clinging to him like a lifeline. "Come on!" he told her. "Enough's enough!" He tugged her in his direction, but Melissa pulled back, holding her ground.

"Where are we going?" she asked, her voice wavering.

Inside the house, the music crescendoed in a horrid assault of sound, like someone had taken a sledgehammer to the piano's keys.

Stone squeezed Melissa's hand, then said firmly, "To put an end to this."

Chapter Thirty-Five

Melissa froze with fear as Stone tugged at her hand. "I don't know if I can."

"You're better off with me," Stone said. "I'm not leaving you out here alone. Not after *that*," he said, viewing the fallen tree.

Melissa nodded numbly, sensing that he was right. She didn't want to be alone, and they were better off together. He led them toward the house with steady steps while Melissa's legs shook. As they approached, the music grew louder. Then, when they were nearly to the stoop, it ceased. Stone stopped and looked over his shoulder, and Melissa's heart stilled. They stood there waiting while wind rustled through the trees and seagulls called. "I think we should go in," Stone whispered.

Melissa clung to his hand and followed him, tracing his steps through the gloomy hallway. Straight in front of her and above the back of Stone's head, Melissa spotted the hand-painted kitchen sign. *May those who come together here, never fall apart.* Deep in the depths of her soul, a switch flipped on and Melissa felt filled with light. This wasn't the first time. Somehow she and Stone had both been here before— together, or at least a part of them had, very long ago.

She tightened her grasp on Stone's hand as he led her through the dining room and into the parlor. The room was perfectly still, save a soft breeze wafting in through the partially opened window. The piano appeared undisturbed, yet the room seemed to vibrate with echoes of sound.

"No!" Stone said. He released her hand and raked his fingers through his hair. "I heard it!" He turned to Melissa with panic-stricken eyes. "We both did."

"Yes," Melissa replied quietly. "I wonder why." Oddly, she was more intrigued than frightened, the warm sense of understanding she'd absorbed in the kitchen having obliterated any fear. Now that she'd experienced a sense of *knowing*, Melissa wanted to explore it more fully. She needed to grasp what everything meant, for her sake—and Stone's. She slowly walked to the piano and laid her hand on the ivories. They were warm to the touch. *Music is the key,* she found herself thinking. The answer to everything at Homecoming Cove. Melissa closed her eyes in quiet meditation, her fingers still on the keys. Then inspiration struck her. It wasn't just about the music. *It was the piano.* The piano that was framed by the gate when viewing it from inside the garden. The piano, which was bookended on one side by the fountain wall at the back of the house...and on the other, by the fallen tree that lay across the driveway in front of the house. Melissa opened her eyes and stared at Stone. "Fiona," she said, catching her breath on the name. "She wasn't trying to hurt me. She was trying to stop me. Stop me from leaving."

Stone stared at her, his expression blank. "But why?"

"The piano," Melissa said urgently, believing she was right. "It's at the center. The center of where the tree fell and where the fountain once stood. And from the rose garden, everything is situated to lead the eye back in here."

Stone turned toward the window, then back toward her. "You can't be saying there's something *in* it?"

Melissa flipped open the top console and began peering inside. "Yes," she said, meeting Stone's gaze. "I think there is." She meticulously examined each wire and hammer while Stone watched her, but after a thorough search she came up with nothing. "Everything appears normal for a piano of this age." Then another idea occurred. "Stone," she said, pointing down, "look in the bench!"

He flipped up the top on the rectangular seat to find a stash of old sheet music. "Only this," he said, holding the pages up in his hands.

"Let me see." Melissa reached out to receive them and Stone simultaneously stepped aside to make room for her to emerge from the corner into which she'd wedged herself. As he did, the backs of his knees knocked the piano bench. He overcorrected, stumbling forward, then tried to right himself, but his footing was unsteady. Stone fell back a step, giving the bench a hard glancing blow before catching himself on the side of the piano to keep from falling. The bench crashed to the floor behind him, splitting apart at its base as its lid hung open. Melissa and Stone stared agape at the small cloth-covered book that had slid out from beneath the piano bench's false bottom and landed on the parlor rug.

"What is it?" Stone asked, amazed.

Melissa bent toward the floor and reached for the journal with trembling fingers. Before she could read the first page, she already knew. "Fiona's diary."

Chapter Thirty-Six

Melissa and Stone sat on the living room sofa. Melissa held Fiona's diary in her hands.

"Are you sure it's okay to read it?" Stone questioned.

"She wanted us to find it," Melissa answered. "I'm sure of it."

After their discovery, the two of them had decided to stay and see what the diary revealed. Stone had returned to their vehicles to quell the engines and remove the keys from the ignitions. In their excitement over Melissa's near miss and the ensuing commotion in the house, they'd left both engines running. Now, all of Melissa's luggage and her groceries languished in the SUV. But it was a brisk fall day. They should keep in the shade a while longer. Relief flooded Melissa as she stared down at the old book. The picture that had been fuzzy all this while was finally coming into focus.

Stone shot her an encouraging look and Melissa cracked the book open. The first thing she saw was musical notation. Lots of it. She thumbed through the pages, finding one handwritten composition after another. "It's her music," Stone said.

"Not just any music." Melissa flipped back to the very first page and glanced at the inside cover of the

book. There, in very elegant penmanship, it read:
Philadelphia Concert Series. "Stone," she told him,
looking up. "This is what we heard…on the records."

"Wow," he said, running a hand across the open
page. "Pretty cool."

Melissa scanned each arrangement, Fiona's music
playing in her head. Yes, this was it exactly. Each of the
pieces she and Stone had heard—except for one. That
was odd. The selection Stone had thought he'd heard
before appeared to be missing. She turned past the final
selection that had been on the album, expecting to find
the absent composition. Instead, she encountered
paragraphs of prose. Melissa drew a hand to her heart.
She'd been right! It was a journal, hidden within the
pages of Fiona's music. "Stone!" she said, breathlessly
reading through sentences. "Listen to this!"

February 3, 1910
It is with great joy in my heart that I write my
Lewis has forgiven me. Yesterday evening, I confessed
everything, and rather than offering a rebuke, he
showered me with kindness. Lewis loves me. I believe
that fully now. In spite of my past. In spite of all that's
gone before…

"Past?" Stone questioned, but Melissa shushed
him, continuing to read.

I told him of my time in Philadelphia and the
events that transpired there. He says I was young,
impetuous, and strong. Strong enough to endure
anything. Which I have. Lewis says we will be a couple
and have a family. He tells me not to hold on to the

past, but it's so very hard. Hard not to think of what I have lost, and can never hold again.

Yesterday evening, lightning raged above the cove, and this morning its waters were choppy, tipping up into furious white points. I begged Lewis not to put out to sea when I saw him off at Port Scarborough, but he insisted with his hearty laugh that he knows how to master the ocean. How many times have I fretted before? And how many times has he come home? An equal number, I admitted shyly, dipping my chin away from his kiss. Now, I wish I hadn't been coy, but had met his lips fully. I'm worried for Lewis so.

The sun has set and he's not yet returned. This is rare, even for when he sails into deep waters. After docking his boat in Port Scarborough, Lewis typically sails his small skiff here. Tonight, he promised to do the same. We'd made plans to discuss the wedding and the short honeymoon trip we'll take afterward. My father patiently waited with me for hours, before eventually retiring to his own home. In June he moved me into this grand house, in which Lewis and I will live as man and wife, and as a birthday gift surprised me with a rose garden. It's a delightful space with a cheerful gurgling fountain, and I can't wait to bring it back in the spring. For now, the bushes huddle low, retreating from the winter winds, and icicles drip from the fountain's basin.

I've had such a bad feeling about Lewis, worrying over the nightmares that have plagued me of late. Of Lewis getting caught up in a squall and his boat going down—though I didn't dare tell him this secret. He'd have called my imagination "overactive" or said I was being dramatic. But no amount of drama can match the painful clench in my heart. Something has gone wrong, and I know it. Just as I feared it would when I gave

Lewis my locket, pressing it yesterday evening into the palm of his hand. The locket belonged to my mother, Marjorie, who died at my birth and whom I've never known. She'd wanted me to have it as a token of her love, and had asked my father to present it to me on my sixteenth birthday, as she might have done had she lived. I'd worn it ever since—before giving it to Lewis, as both a good luck charm and a token of the trust between us. Only Lewis knows how special my locket is and its true sentimental value, which is why he was reluctant to take it.

"If you insist on going tomorrow, at least take this with you." He glanced down at it and then said, "Your most precious possession." "No," I replied, covering his heart with my hand, "my most precious possession dwells here."

Melissa stopped reading to wipe back a tear, and saw Stone's eyes had reddened.

"She knew, didn't she?" he asked hoarsely. "Fiona had a sense that something bad was going to happen."

"But Lewis wouldn't listen," Melissa agreed. "He was headstrong."

"Sounds like Fiona was too."

"She gave him her locket. He was supposed to take it with him."

"But he didn't," Stone replied. "He probably didn't want to risk losing it. If the weather became rough, or the sea got choppy...Lewis couldn't take the chance." Stone shut his eyes, remembering his dream and the fine chain floating through the water. It would have been the last thing of Fiona's Lewis would have seen, the last connection to her he might have held. "He left it behind in his memory box for safekeeping." He stared down at the book. "Is there more?"

Melissa shook her head. "Not in this entry, no. It's like she stopped writing abruptly. Near the bottom of the page, some of the ink is blurred and the paper appears pockmarked, as if by raindrops or—"

Stone's face fell in understanding. "Tears."

"I wonder what made the locket so special," Melissa said. "I mean, apart from the fact that it was left to Fiona by her mother. Somehow, it seems Fiona was hinting there was something more. Something that only Lewis understood."

"Maybe she explains it later?"

Melissa carefully searched through the journal's pages, her frown deepening. "There's nothing else here about the locket. These entries are all about Fiona awaiting Lewis's return. She mentions standing on the dock and the cold snows coming…feeling taken by a fever…" Melissa pursed her lips and shut the book.

"I'm sorry, Melissa." Stone took her hand. "I know it's hard. Hard even reading about it. Poor Fiona."

"Poor Lewis," Melissa said.

They exchanged heartbroken glances, each of them intuiting how Fiona and Lewis must have felt. Lewis, when he hit that final moment and understood he'd never be coming home. And Fiona, when she realized that the love of her life had been lost. All at once, any sense of peril was lifted and Stone felt nothing but overwhelming sadness. "You were never really in danger, were you?" he asked Melissa.

"From Fiona?" she answered. "No, I don't believe that I was. It was more like…she was trying to get my attention."

"She seemed to want both of ours," Stone said.

"Yes," Melissa replied. "But why?" She cast her eyes over Fiona's journal as if it might offer up answers, yet the book sat silently in her hands. "I wish there was a way to know what had happened in Philadelphia," Melissa said. "That seemed to play a very big part is something she confessed to Lewis."

"I'm guessing she played a concert there. The entire series is on those records and in her journal."

"Not the entire series…" Melissa suddenly set Fiona's book on the coffee table. "Stone," she said confidently. "One piece is missing from this collection, a piece that played on the records."

"How do you know?"

"It was the one you thought you'd heard before. The sweet one that sounded like a child's lullaby. I found it particularly odd that such an endearing piece would have such a sad name. When I switched out the records, the title caught my eye."

Stone gazed at her expectantly.

"It was called 'Heartbreak.'"

Chapter Thirty-Seven

Melissa returned to the parlor and opened the piano bench that Stone had straightened after its fall. She lifted the lid, found the recessed lever at the far left, and slid back its false bottom. Just as she'd suspected, another small book lay underneath. Its pages were splayed open and had become wedged in the mechanism that held the false bottom track. When the other volume had slipped out, this one had been hung up inside. They hadn't seen it, as they'd assumed the first book to be the only hidden treasure. This one was much thinner, and had a small stitched binding with a thick cardboard cover painted with roses on either side. *Roses, of course, for Fiona.* Melissa's eyes trailed to the window and took in the rose garden. Its gate was once again ajar, flapping back and forth in the breeze.

"You found a second book!" Stone proclaimed from the doorway. He'd followed her, but she'd worked quickly in uncovering her new prize.

"Yes," Melissa said, gently parting it with her fingers. She gazed down at the delicate penmanship before her, then carefully scanned through the modest collection of pages. "This one is much shorter and mostly in prose. There's only one song in here."

"'Heartbreak,'" Stone guessed correctly.

Back in the living room, Melissa and Stone pored through the new volume's pages, and the entry they found on page five astounded them.

March 2, 1907
I've met a fine gentleman in Philadelphia named Jeremy Ashton. He appeared backstage holding a tall hat and wearing a broad, mustached smile. The roses I'd received earlier were from him. In fact, every rose bouquet I've received this week has been his secret offering. Jeremy sent roses of nearly every color and size, each of them blooming with succulent sweetness. How did he know they are my weakness, I wonder?

"There was someone before Lewis," Melissa gasped with surprise.
"Keep reading," Stone urged.
Melissa flipped through a few more pages.

Jeremy owns one of the fine hotels in this grand city. He's arranged a room for me on the top floor: the Ambassador Suite, he called it. And now I know why. He's using it to diplomatically petition my affections. Every day there is a new gift, each one wildly extravagant. Jeremy even had the concierge deliver a peacock on Tuesday, and all because I said I'd never seen one. My heart races to think a man of such stature could pay such generous attention to me.
My chaperone, Liza, has taken to his butler, Tim, a younger man who seems to accompany Jeremy everywhere and tend to his most miniscule needs. Lately, Tim has been entertaining Liza in the lobby with card games and conversation, while Jeremy courts me

privately. Jeremy has professed his love to me, and has promised we will marry. I confess he has captured my heart.

"Quite the opposite of Lewis," Stone commented from beside her on the sofa. "Worldly…wealthy…"

"And married," Melissa cut in.

"What?" Stone furrowed his brow. "What makes you think Jeremy was married?"

"This," she said, staring down at the next page.

March 13, 1907

I am torn apart, my very soul wrenched from my body. I cannot breathe, nor dare to trust my reckless heart with emotion. Oh, how foolish I have been. What a silly, stupid girl, believing that Jeremy could be mine. Today, I caught him by surprise on the street in passing. He was arm in arm with his wife, an elegant lady holding a dazzling parasol. Behind them trailed two finely dressed children, both girls with shiny blond ringlets and angelic blue eyes. Jeremy has a wife and family. He came to the hotel later this evening and lambasted me for nearly giving him away, for practically ruining everything. How could I even think there was more to he and I than a simple lovers' game?

Tomorrow, my Philadelphia tour is ending, and I can't wait to move far away. Far away from this city to which I hope never to return. Hot humiliation burns through me. Thank goodness this is our secret alone. One belonging to me and Jeremy. I don't believe even Tim and Liza have been aware. One thing is sure, I will never again give my heart so freely. Perhaps I shall never give it to anyone ever again, but hold it safe inside me, where it can reside in peace and solitude always, without the horrid, tainted memories of what might have been.

Melissa stared at Stone in astonishment.

"I had no idea about any of that," he said.

"How could you? How could anyone know?"

"It doesn't sound like she told a soul before Lewis," Stone replied.

"And when she did, he completely understood and forgave her."

"Of course he did. When a man loves a woman…" Stone looked right into Melissa's soul. "He'd forgive her almost anything."

"It doesn't sound like she'd even met Lewis then."

"That's right," Stone said. "They met after she'd settled permanently here with her father, after she'd given up touring."

"Do you think that was because of Jeremy?" Melissa wondered.

Stone gazed out the window at the cove, where early evening was settling in, casting shadows over the water. "I don't know."

Melissa started to put the journal aside, but something inside it caught her attention. The tip of some satiny fabric poked out from between two pages at the back of the book. When she pulled the pages apart, Melissa saw that what she had noticed wasn't fabric at all, but a dried red rose petal. It marked a special spot in the journal, one pointing to Fiona's most painful memory. "Stone!" Melissa inhaled sharply, then her jaw dropped open. "Fiona was pregnant."

Melissa passed Stone the book in a trance, her mind beginning to whirl. "Please read it."

Stone surveyed her features, not understanding, yet also somehow sensing a phenomenal revelation was about to occur. He slowly lifted the journal in his hand and read aloud.

November 29, 1907
Today I died a thousand deaths when they took away my baby. They wrenched him from my arms while I cried and screamed and begged them to let him stay. But this is the way it's always done, a kindly midwife told me. He will go on to a group home now. If he is lucky he will find a family. But he has a family! I protested in a screech. He's my flesh and blood! It was as if no one could hear me, or nobody cared. They threatened to tie me to the bed if I went after him. I can't fathom my father arranging this, nor that he could condone such savagery by sending me to the Home for Wayward Girls in New York. Clearly, he must not have understood. Surely, he couldn't have known it would come to this. My own father couldn't deceive me.

Stone stopped reading and looked up. "What an awful betrayal for Fiona."

"Women didn't have babies out of wedlock in those days," Melissa replied grimly. "At least not that the rest of society was aware of."

"Things were glossed over, covered up," Stone said.

"Poor Fiona was worldly thanks to her music, but she was still naïve. It sounds like she didn't know what her father had in mind when he sent her away. I can't imagine the horror she felt when she had her child taken from her."

"After being crushed by that whirlwind affair," Stone added.

Melissa speculated on another truth. "Perhaps that, in part, was why Fiona's father built her such a grand house, later. He was trying to make amends for what had gone before."

"By building Fiona and Lewis this amazing place here."

"Keep reading," Melissa said plaintively, compassion etched on her face.

December 13, 1907
I am packing today to leave the girls' home. I will have a word with my father when I return to Virginia, and together we will find my son. Find my son and bring him back to his rightful family, and to me. I've made the acquaintance of a kindly young woman here, and she's vowed to help me. Penelope assists one of the midwives and is still a girl herself. She too was forced to give up her baby, and fully understands the pain of it. Penelope also saw me in concert, one time in New York, and believes a terrible injustice has been done to someone she calls a "fine musician." Penelope says she has ways to look into records and perhaps track my baby down. As soon as she does, she will let me know his whereabouts.

I don't care that the baby's father can never be a part of things, and it appears he has no interest in stepping forward. For the first few months of my pregnancy, I tried to reach him, but Jeremy ignored my correspondence. Ultimately, he began returning my letters unread. Or perhaps he had Tim return them for him. For this reason, Jeremy will never know that I've written one more piece for the Philadelphia collection.

When the album is recorded, I'll see that this new number is included, even though it was never in the original concert program. I'll place it midway in the series, so no one can suspect that it was actually written later. Most will simply assume it was omitted from the concert program, perhaps for being too maudlin. My new piece is called "Heartbreak" and it was written for my baby. Now, each time I play it, or someone hears it on my record, it will serve as a tribute to my little son. I will find him, I will, just as soon as my time up north is done. With Penelope's assistance or without it, although I pray she will endeavor to help me.

Following my stay at the girls' home, my father has arranged for me to make phonographic recordings of the Philadelphia series with a music producer in Camden, New Jersey. Everyone in Virginia has been told that's what I've been doing all along. As gramophone recording is new and people assume it to be an arduous process, no one will question the time frame of my being away. I can't wait to be done with the stupid album and find my child. My father has said that I'll never tour again, because he won't allow it. And I don't intend to fight him. All I want is to be a mother to my child. If I chased after him now, they might lock me away in an asylum. Then what good would I do my baby boy? Much better to play the game, and return coolly to Virginia, where I can speak to my father in a newly adult way. Perhaps he will listen. Perhaps he will hear me out. Perhaps my most precious possession will be returned to his mother's arms.

Melissa clutched her hands to her mouth and Stone stopped reading. "Melissa? What is it?"

"*My most precious possession.* Those were the words Fiona used to describe her locket." She glanced at him urgently. "Do you still have it?"

"In my pocket, yes." He fished for it and extracted it, dangling it toward her in his fingers. It spun and sparkled in the fading daylight.

Melissa took it from him and, as she did, the book that had been resting on her knees slid to the floor. Stone reached for it, his eyes glued to an open page. "Melissa, wait!" he said with urgency. "There's more!" He thumbed quickly through some pages, then turned back to the spot that had caught his eye. "Listen to this."

August 2, 1908

Today, I heard from Penelope. My heart raced and my fingers trembled as I opened her letter. How my heart hoped that my prayers, at last, would be answered. Every line of inquiry I'd tried on my own had either come to a dead end or been blocked by my father, who encouraged me to leave the past behind and instead focus on the future. But what future could I envision without my baby boy? Perhaps Penelope's luck had been better.

I began reading her note filled with hope, but then my heart sank like an anchor. For the news Penelope sent of my son led me to believe that perhaps my father had been right. Penelope shared that little Benjamin has been adopted by a loving couple, who were unable to have a child of their own. The husband is a solid tradesman, while the wife is a woman of means who comes from a wealthy family. Her family apparently opposed the marriage, but softened immediately upon adoption of the baby. They help support the couple in a handsome home, complete with domestic help, including a full-time nanny.

Penelope reports that she met with them and they appear to be taking exceptional care of Benjamin. What's more, they seem to deeply love him, and it's apparent the infant responds to their affection. Perhaps the most telling gesture was one made by the adoptive mother when she learned I was inquiring after my child. She opened the locket that dangled from around her neck and removed a small photograph of the baby. "Please give this to the mother," she urged Penelope, "and tell her that little Benjamin is being well looked after. We love him, we do, and can't thank her enough for her generosity in helping our hearts' desire come true." Tears leaked from my eyes at her kindness, and also when I realized they'd kept the baby's given name, the one I had anointed him with in the home. Although, Penelope reports they changed his surname to align with theirs, as they intend to raise him as their son, and as if he were naturally born into their family.

I knew upon reading Penelope's letter that I could never tear that family apart. Not in a selfish effort to restore my own, broken as it would be. What kind of mother would that make me? The sort who puts her own needs above the welfare of her son? Little Benjamin is better off with these new people in New York. He will have both a mother and a father there, and will escape the stigma of being raised as a bastard child in Virginia.

And so it is—with a shattered heart—I've decided to finally let my baby go. Go into a much brighter future than I myself could offer him in this tiny town on the Eastern Shore. He has a new life and a new surname provided to him by his adoptive parents, but in my heart he'll always stay mine.

"Stone," Melissa said suddenly. "Fiona was given a locket-size photo of her child." She popped open the locket in her hand, exposing the faded baby photograph. "I don't think this picture is of Fiona," she said seriously. "It's of her *most precious possession*: her son."

"But the dress is so frilly."

"That's how infant boys were dressed in those days," Melissa explained. She dug her fingernail under the fine rim of the frame holding the picture.

"What are you doing?" Stone asked her.

"I want to see if anything's written on the back."

"Like what?"

Melissa carefully slid the photo out of the bracket that held it and lifted it gingerly between her thumb and index finger. "Like this," she said softly, reading two initials. "It says *B. C.*"

"*B.* for Benjamin," Stone guessed, "and *C.* for…?"

Melissa spotted a small piece of paper that had been tucked behind the photograph's locket frame and pried it out with her fingers. She folded it open, her hands shaking. When she saw the words written there, tears sprang from her eyes.

Stone laid a steadying hand on her arm and Melissa's heart pounded.

"It says…" Her voice quavered. "Benjamin Carter…"

"Carter?" Stone questioned. "Like *your family's* Carter?"

Melissa nodded as tears streamed down her cheeks and she finished reading. "Son of Emmet and Calista Carter, born November 29, 1907."

Stone locked on Melissa's gaze, waiting for her to continue.

"My great-grandfather on my dad's side was Benjamin Carter. His parents were Emmet and Calista. I never knew he'd been adopted. Emmet and Calista must have played that close to the vest. Perhaps only their parents knew. I don't believe Benjamin himself was ever aware. They completely raised him as their own."

Her lips quivered and her voice broke apart. Melissa suddenly found herself weeping. Could this really be true? Could she be directly descended from Fiona? She'd spent all her life in New York, had researched her family tree...had believed herself wholly aware of every ancestor, and yet this detail had escaped her.

She set the tiny photo and the unfolded piece of paper beside the locket on the coffee table, trying to catch her breath, but the sobs kept coming. "Stone," she said through her tears. "I've researched my family's records. My relative Benjamin Carter's birthday was November 29, 1907."

Stone's Adam's apple rose and fell, the truth sinking in. "You're related to Fiona," he said, stunned.

Melissa met his eyes. "Fiona's secret baby was my great-grandfather."

"That makes Fiona—?"

"My great-great-grandmother." She drew a deep breath and released it. "Exactly."

Chapter Thirty-Eight

Stone wrapped his arms around Melissa and pulled her close to him on the sofa. He glanced out the windows at the cove, watching dusk shroud its waters. Shadows filled the room around them and Stone felt the urge to build a fire. But that could wait. For now, Melissa needed to be held. It was mind-blowing to think Melissa was descended from Fiona, just as Stone was related to Lewis. Fiona and Lewis had shared a certain destiny, yet their future together had been cut short. Now, generations later, Fiona and Lewis were having their chance again—through Melissa and Stone. But what about Fiona and her turmoil? Would Melissa and Stone knowing the truth about her past put Fiona's spirit to rest, or was there something more that had to be accomplished? Stone rested his chin on the top of Melissa's head and held her tightly, shutting his eyes. An image of Fiona's locket drifted through the darkness before him. Stone thought of Lewis, and that fine gold chain floating above him just out of reach in the water. Stone opened his eyes and spoke hoarsely. "Melissa," he said with assurance. "Fiona's locket! I know what we need to do!"

She lifted her head off his shoulder to gaze at him. "What is it?"

"It's Lewis," Stone answered. "He was meant to have this."

"I know, and Fiona gave it to him. It was a token of the trust between them, because she'd told Lewis about Benjamin. The locket was doubly precious to Fiona, so it was the most valuable thing she could offer Lewis besides her heart."

"But he left the locket in the memory box," Stone said urgently, "instead of carrying it with him as Fiona intended." Stone stared into Melissa's sea-blue eyes. "Fiona's not the only one who's been restless," he said. "Lewis has been troubled too."

Her delicate brow rose. "The dream?"

Stone nodded. "But it wasn't me in the water—"

"It was Lewis," she said, reiterating what the two of them had discussed earlier.

"And this…" Stone lifted Fiona's locket off the coffee table and dangled it from its chain. "Was always just out of reach."

Melissa gently pushed away and sat upright on the sofa. "You think Lewis regrets not taking it with him?"

"I believe he does," Stone answered. "It was a memento he was supposed to keep close to his heart. Fiona trusted that it would keep him safe."

"But he let her down," Melissa responded.

"Though totally without meaning to. I'm sure Lewis didn't want to lose the locket at sea. That's why he left it at home."

"This is Lewis's unfinished business," Melissa said with understanding. "It's doubtful the locket could have saved his life, but when his last thoughts were of Fiona…when he realized his ship was going under…he probably wished that he had it."

"As a last desperate attempt to hold on to her," Stone said in agreement.

"Maybe that's been what's blocking them from being together," Melissa said. "Lewis's guilt over the locket—and his heartbreak at leaving Fiona behind."

"Fiona wanted us to know," Stone answered. "I feel sure of it."

"Just like she wanted us to find each other."

Stone met her gaze. "Yes. We were wrong to think she was trying to interfere. Fiona wanted us together. Everything that's happened here, all of the disturbances, were just Fiona's way of trying to get her message across."

"About who I really am," Melissa answered.

Stone nodded solemnly. "And the importance of the locket."

Melissa looked out at the cove, then down at Fiona's locket. "Stone," she said softly, scanning his eyes. "Are you thinking what I am?"

"Your dream about the boat—and your walking out onto the dock...that had something to do with this."

"In my dream, I was thinking, *Finally we'll be together.*"

"You mean, that Fiona and Lewis would."

"Yes. I...I mean, she...was driven toward the water, Stone. There's something there that's meant to unite them."

"It's not entirely about Homecoming Cove," Stone said. "The missing link lies in the palm of my hand." He contemplated this a moment, then closed his fingers around the locket. "We need to do what Fiona intended. Send her most precious possession to where it belongs."

"With Lewis."

Stone stood and held out his hand. Melissa took it, and he lifted her to her feet.

"What about the museum?" Melissa questioned. "This is such a special piece."

"This piece was never meant for a museum," Stone said. "I think we both know that."

She nodded and Stone handed her the jacket she'd set on a nearby chair when they'd settled in to read Fiona's journals. Melissa slipped into it and Stone pulled on his coat as well, then he slid Benjamin's photo and the piece of paper back in the locket. "Let's go," he said. "Before I change my mind."

While Stone believed this was the right thing to do, he also regretted letting this special family memento go. Yet, deep in his heart, Stone understood Fiona's locket really wasn't his to keep. It was always meant for Lewis. He could tell Melissa was thinking the same things as they made their way outdoors and walked toward the dock, hand in hand.

Wind rustled through the trees around the cove and the sun sank low, giving a golden glow to the water. "Stone," Melissa said. "I have a sense about this. It's like having the feeling that this is where we're supposed to be, and what we're meant to do."

Stone squeezed her hand. "Yes."

They stepped onto the dock and traversed its length, striding confidently toward its furthermost end. The wind picked up, rippling the water around them. Stone lifted the hand holding the locket and Melissa gently asked him, "Can I see it one last time?"

She took it and popped it open, staring fondly at the baby's picture. Then she snapped the locket shut and raised it to her lips, giving it a soft kiss. "Rest well, Lewis and Fiona," she said quietly before returning the locket to Stone. He smiled warmly and followed her example, kissing the locket gently as well. "It's time," he said, meeting her eyes. "Time to lay the past to rest."

Melissa pressed her lips together as heat blurred her eyes.

Stone firmly grasped the locket, then threw back his arm before lobbing it forward in a long shot. The glittering locket with its trailing chain sailed through the air in a high arc and plunked down far away on the water, just at the point where the cove opened up into the river and rushing currents ran deep. Stone's eyes followed the flow of the tide as it raced toward the bay, where it would eventually meet the Atlantic. "So long, Fiona," he said under his breath.

Just then, a fierce burst of wind lifted off the cove and behind them something loudly clanked shut. Melissa and Stone turned toward the house to see the wavering garden gate had closed on its own and now sat firmly latched in place. The house beyond it was suddenly awash with warm light, Fiona's piano just visible through the parlor window.

Melissa blinked as a tear escaped her. "It's done now, isn't it?"

Stone stared down into her beautiful blue eyes and held her close, understanding that this chapter in their lives was finished. "Yes, my love," he said. "It's done."

Chapter Thirty-Nine

Stone kept his arm around Melissa's shoulders as they returned to the house. He stared up at the structure with its classic Virginia farmhouse lines and broad back porch, thinking how much he wanted to make it his. Before, Stone had never been sure of the timing. Perhaps now the timing was right. While the house had been kept up, there was still so much he could do to restore it to its original glory. If Melissa were living here with him, he'd have added incentive to make everything perfect. But, that was in the future. At present, a heavy oak lay sideways across the driveway, blocking Melissa's path to the road. While it was already late, Stone could still pull out his chainsaw and remove it, making way for Melissa's retreat. Yet Stone wasn't prepared for Melissa to leave. "It's getting dark out," he said. "Might not be the best time to start off on a long drive."

"No," Melissa agreed, snuggling against him as they moved along. "It might be best to wait until morning."

"Or maybe the morning after that… Melissa." Stone stopped walking and took her hand. "I don't want you to go. Now that things are…" He hesitated on the word. "...settled here, don't you think you can stay a little longer?"

She looked up at him and smiled softly. "I'd like that. I would like to stay a while...and get to know you better."

"I think you know me pretty well as it is. Truth is, I think you know me better than any other woman ever has."

Melissa's words were hushed. "And you probably know me better than any other guy."

"You and me...and Homecoming Cove..." His voice was raspy above the wind. "We were brought together for a reason. At least that's how I feel." His fingers tightened around hers. "Do you believe that too?"

She answered by standing up on her tiptoes and giving his mouth a soft kiss. "What do you think?" she whispered.

"I think you feel what I feel," Stone answered.

"Then you know I love you too."

Stone's spirit soared and his heart hammered harder. "You make me the happiest man alive," he said huskily. "Only one thing could make me happier."

Her big blue eyes went wide.

"Knowing you were coming to live here permanently," Stone continued. "In this house with me."

Her smile was a ray of sunshine in the darkening afternoon. "Are you asking me to—?"

"Marry me, Melissa," he said boldly. "Marry me and come live by my side. Be my helpmate, partner, and friend in restoring this old place and building the museum. In return, I'll be there for you and support your music. Whatever your heart desires, I'll make it yours. Because nobody—I mean, no other woman on earth—completely takes my breath away like you do. No one could even come close."

For an impossibly long moment she gazed at him. Then suddenly tears filled her eyes. "You leave me pretty breathless too."

Stone grinned. "But in a good way, yeah?"

Melissa released a long, happy sigh. "In the best possible way."

Stone tugged her up against him and ran his fingers through her hair, cradling her head in his hands. "If you don't answer me, woman," he said hungrily, "I think I'll go crazy."

Melissa laughed and squeezed him up against her. "Yes, Stone. I'll marry you. There's nobody else's wife I'd rather be."

Stone lowered his mouth toward hers. "You won't be afraid to live here?"

Her face was awash with joy. "I already consider it my home."

Stone kissed her deeply then, as autumn winds circled around them. He couldn't imagine anything finer than being married to Melissa and living with her at Homecoming Cove. His happiest dreams were about to come true.

Chapter Forty

Melissa and Stone were still kissing ten minutes later when a coarse older voice cut in.

"Well, I beg your pardon!"

The couple broke apart to find Captain Bill standing by the door to the screened porch, holding a grocery store bouquet of flowers. "Captain Bill!" Melissa cried in surprise, smoothing down her hair.

Stone turned toward the old man with a questioning look. "Grandpa?"

"Saw that tree down out front," Captain Bill said, his pipe clenched between his teeth. "And that mess of rubble over there." He motioned toward the ruined fountain wall in the garden. "Just what in the blazes has been going on around here? Everybody okay?"

Melissa and Stone exchanged glances and Melissa felt her cheeks burn. "We're fine," she said. "Just—"

"Better than fine." Stone tugged her toward him in a one-arm hug. "Melissa and I are getting married."

Bill removed the pipe from his teeth to let out a whistle. "That so?" His expression was cloudy at first, but then it brightened. "How did this happen?"

"It's a long story," Stone answered.

"I got the time," Bill said.

Melissa smiled warmly and addressed Bill. "Why don't you stay for dinner? We'll explain everything over a glass of wine."

"Might take a whole bottle," Stone said, chuckling.

Bill stared at them, perplexed. "Well, all right. If you'll have me..." He glanced at Melissa. "That would be very nice. Oh, hey!" he said, striding toward her. "Nearly forgot. These are for you."

"For me?" Melissa asked, surprised.

"Came by to apologize," Bill said deferentially. "For, um...potentially misreading things." He surveyed the couple before him quizzically, as if thinking he might not have misread them at all. Stone slowly shook his head and everybody laughed.

"Thank you," Melissa said, taking the flowers. "That was very kind." She looked down at the bouquet, seeing he'd brought her roses. "These were Fiona's favorites."

"Were they?" Bill asked.

"We've got a lot to tell you about Fiona," Stone said.

"And Lewis," Melissa added.

"Looks like you'll need some assistance getting that luggage out of your SUV first," Bill replied.

Melissa grinned. "That would be a huge help."

Bill tucked his pipe into his pocket. "My pleasure." He headed into the house and Melissa and Stone followed him. As they did, Stone took Melissa's hand.

"I plan to put in a bid on this house tomorrow."

"Tomorrow?" Melissa asked, delighted. "Are you...able to do that?"

"Sweetheart," he said with a grin. "Those ten years in the Caribbean made me a very rich man."

Melissa gasped with happy surprise and Stone winked.

"No sense waiting, as far as I can see. Might as well get the purchase done, so I can get started on improvements and repairs. You and I can talk over the timing of your move—and our wedding," he added cheerfully, "when you're ready."

"*Our wedding*," Melissa said dreamily. "I like the sound of that." She turned to look at Stone. "When should we have it? What time of year?"

"I was thinking of the summer, when roses are in bloom..."

Melissa envisioned Fiona's garden with a fully functioning fountain and fragrant, blossoming bushes. "An outdoor wedding at Homecoming Cove?" Melissa smiled brightly, her heart bounding. "I love that idea, Stone. I absolutely love it. I do."

"Good," he said, giving her a kiss. "Then I love it too."

Epilogue

Five Years Later

Melissa adjusted the wide brim of her sun hat and gazed across the top of the white picket fence toward the water. Four-year-old William stood happily by his dad, staring up at Stone with admiring eyes. Stone was bent down on one knee and carefully instructing the child on the nuances of baiting a hook. Though Melissa had worried William was too young for fishing, Stone had assured her that he himself had gotten started at that age. All it took was careful supervision, which Stone was glad to provide. Melissa smiled fondly at the pair, thinking what a terrific dad Stone made.

He'd done a marvelous job opening the museum, and had become quite a town celebrity for benefiting local tourism. Now that the mariner's museum was up and running, Stone had appointed Captain Bill to serve as docent. This relieved Bill, who was getting elderly, of the more arduous handiwork around here that Stone had eagerly taken on shortly after buying the place. The fields had been replanted and sweet summer corn was nearly ripe for picking. And this gorgeous rose garden was once again in its prime, thanks to Stone's loving restoration of the fountain and Melissa's tender care of the blossoms.

She inhaled deeply, savoring the intoxicating scent wafting on the breeze, and turned toward the parlor window framing the piano. Since she'd moved to Homecoming Cove, Melissa's career had flourished. She'd received assignment after assignment, and had reached the point where she could pick and choose among offers, dovetailing her work in nicely with raising her family. Melissa laid a hand on her big, round belly, and her heart swelled with happiness. William would have a baby sister soon, and their family would be complete. Melissa couldn't imagine anything more wonderful than her life at Homecoming Cove. "How's it going over there?" she called to Stone and William by the water.

Stone turned her way and smiled. "Everything's just great!" He shot her a mock captain's salute, and Melissa grinned happily, so at peace with her life and her world. She believed that Fiona and Lewis were also at peace, and was thankful she and Stone had played a part in allowing their spirits to finally rest. Melissa and Stone hadn't experienced any further disturbances since casting Fiona's locket out to sea. Stone's troubling nightmares had also ceased. He now claimed to dream only of her.

Melissa delighted in drifting off to sleep each night in Stone's loving embrace, with him holding her close, just as he'd done during their first night together. Stone had a way of making Melissa feel safe, and cared for...and cherished. Melissa couldn't possibly love any man more. Nor could she imagine any finer place to live. She gazed around the grounds, contentment settling inside her. It was a life she might never have expected, but one that was filled with promise and never-ending joy. Out here, on the isolated Virginia Eastern Shore, Melissa's heart had come home.

The End

A Note from the Author

Thanks for reading *The House at Homecoming Cove*. I hope you enjoyed it. If you did, please help other people find this book.

1. This book is lendable, so send it to a friend you think might like it so that she (or he) can discover my work too.

2. Help other people find this book: Write a review.

3. Sign up for my newsletter so you can learn about the next book as soon as it's available. Write to GinnyBairdRomance@gmail.com with "newsletter" in the subject heading.

4. Come like my Facebook page: https://www.facebook.com/GinnyBairdRomance.

5. Connect with me on Twitter: https://twitter.com/GinnyBaird.

6. Visit my website at http://www.ginnybairdromance.com for details on other books now available at multiple outlets.

If you enjoy sweet, mysterious love stories with a slightly spooky edge, you might like the other two books in the Romantic Ghost Stories Series, *The Ghost Next Door (A Love Story)* and *The Light at the End of the Road*. An excerpt from each novel follows.

The Ghost Next Door (A Love Story)
A single mom and her teenage daughter move next to a spooky old house, and the small-town sheriff comes to their aid.

Chapter One

Elizabeth set her hand on her hip and gazed out over the countryside. She and Claire stood by their silver SUV, parked at the top of the steep gravel drive.

"Thought you said it had a view."

She glanced at the fifteen-year-old girl beside her with long, brown hair and bangs. Dark eyes brimmed with dramatic expression.

"Jeez, Mom. You didn't say it was of a graveyard."

"Cemetery."

"What?"

"Graveyards are beside a church. Cemeteries are stand-alone—"

Claire's jaw dropped in disbelief. "If you're such a stickler for words, why didn't you read the fine print?"

"What fine print?"

"The one saying we'd be moving next to a haunted house?"

Elizabeth's gaze traveled to the run-down Victorian less than a stone's throw from the modern, prefab house they'd rented. She figured the land the newer house stood on had once belonged to the larger home, which now sat with murky windows, sunshine reflecting off of beveled glass. Its wide front porch was caked with dust, gnarly vines tangling their way around paint-cracked spindles holding the porch railings.

Elizabeth chided herself for not investigating further when the ad said Bucolic, small-town setting. Unobstructed mountain views. She hadn't known those views would be peppered with tombstones, or that they'd be living beside an empty house.

"Maybe it won't be so bad?" she offered hopefully.

A sharp wind blew, sending the twin rockers on the Victorian's front porch sighing as they heaved to and fro as if tipped by some unseen hand.

Claire frowned, turning away. "It's creepy. This whole place is creepy. I don't think we should stay."

A tension in Elizabeth's gut told her perhaps Claire was right. Even the rocking chairs tilting in the wind seemed a bad omen. But a greater tension in her wallet said she'd already signed a lease for the next nine months. There'd be no backing out of it without losing her security deposit plus the first month's rent.

Elizabeth drew a breath, studying the more positive parts of the landscape. The two-story place they'd rented appeared almost new, with a cheery front garden and a covered stoop. Its clapboard siding and slate roof were well kept, giving the home a cottagey feel. And the large side yard housed a sturdy oak, its leaves shimmering orangey gold in the October sun. "The setting may be a little unusual," she told her daughter, "but at least it's quiet."

"Yeah. Dead quiet."

"Come on," Elizabeth urged. "Help me get the groceries in the house. Then we can grab our luggage. We'll be settled in no time." She flashed the girl a grin. "Spaghetti for dinner."

Claire shrugged and reluctantly reached into the hatchback for some bags. "Whatever."

Later that night, as she and Claire stood drying dishes by the sink, Elizabeth questioned her wisdom in bringing them here. This rental property was pretty isolated, at least five miles from the tiny village nearby. But when she'd been searching for a temporary place for them to stay, there hadn't been a lot of options. Blayton, Virginia was so small it wasn't even on most maps. Set up against the Blue Ridge Mountains, it had once been an old railroad town, the gateway community between here and Tennessee on the far side of those high peaks. After a period of anonymity, it was now undergoing a minor renaissance, with a new microbrewery moving in, a few swank restaurants, and a burgeoning host of surrounding vineyards and upscale B&Bs. Though trains no longer stopped here, the working tracks remained intact, with the original station now converted into the local library.

Elizabeth had been sent here to revamp the old town newspaper, previously called the Gazette. Her larger news organization was intent on acquiring antiquated or defunct town papers and bringing their newer incarnations into the twenty-first century. Elizabeth had fought this relocation, begging her boss in Richmond to let her tackle this from afar. After all, the real focus of all their newer editions was virtual subscriptions offered on the Internet. But Jerry had argued she needed to be on the scene, get up close and personal with the local community to make this transition work. Besides, he persisted, in order for the new publication to be successful, it needed to develop ground legs too. Perhaps a younger readership might emerge online, but for the old-timers to get roped in, there had to be a physical edition of the paper as well. Something folks could pick up at the local grocery, which was extra convenient since there was only one store in town.

"Mom, look!" Claire's eyes went wide as the dish she was drying slipped from her hands. It collided with the linoleum at her feet and split in two.

Elizabeth stepped toward her daughter. "Honey, what's wrong?"

"Did… Did you see it?" Claire stammered.

She followed Claire's gaze out the kitchen window to the house across the way. Evening shadows shrouded the Victorian, its windows dark and dreary.

"Up there." She pointed to a window on the second floor. "I saw something move inside."

Elizabeth wrapped her arm around Claire's shoulder, thinking the day was getting to her. It had been a five-hour drive from Richmond, then there'd been unpacking to do. It was unnerving to be a teen and move far from your school and long-term friends. It had to be doubly upsetting to find your new home situated across the street from a cemetery. The poor kid was tired and overwrought, letting her imagination get the best of her. And Claire had quite an imagination. She'd taken first prize in her district's teen short-story contest and had recently turned her storytelling ability into songwriting while she plucked out accompanying music on her secondhand guitar.

"I'm sure it was nothing," Elizabeth told her. "Maybe just a shadow from the big oak outside."

Claire narrowed her eyes in thought. "Yeah, maybe." She bent to grab the broken dish, and Elizabeth stooped to help her.

"Here, let me get this. Why don't you go grab the broom and dustpan from over there in the corner?"

After the two of them had cleaned up, they once more stood by the sink and stared out the window.

"I'm sure it was just a shadow," Elizabeth said.

"You're probably right."

Just then a beam of light swept through the big house's downstairs, and Claire leapt into Elizabeth's arms. "Mo-om!"

Elizabeth held her tightly. "Hang on, I'm sure it's just a—"

"A what?" Elizabeth's pulse raced. "You said the house was empty! For sale!"

"Maybe it's a potential buyer?" Elizabeth said lamely, not for a second believing that was true. Who on earth visited creepy old houses as night fell? Maybe someone who worked during the day and couldn't get here otherwise, Elizabeth told herself logically. Just look at her, gripping her daughter like she was some freaked-out kid herself. Elizabeth knew better than that.

"Is it gone?" Claire asked, her eyes tightly shut.

Elizabeth returned her gaze to the window and the looming house next door. There wasn't a hint of movement anywhere. "No signs of life."

Claire popped both eyes open. "I wish you hadn't said that."

Just then the doorbell rang with a spooky twang, and Elizabeth yelped.

"Ow, Mom! What are you doing? It's just the front door."

Elizabeth released her grasp, feeling foolish. "Of course it is," she replied in an even tone. But they weren't expecting company and were miles from anywhere.

The doorbell chimed again, and Claire strode in that direction.

"Where are you going?"

"To answer it."

"Wait." Elizabeth protectively stepped in front of her. "Better let me." She was fairly sure ghosts didn't ring doorbells. But it certainly couldn't be a neighbor bringing cookies.

Nathan Thorpe stood on the stoop of the cozy house, holding a brimming plate wrapped in tinfoil. Walnut-chocolate chip. His specialty. He'd heard the new people had moved in and wanted to welcome them to town. Blayton didn't get many visitors. Full-fledged transplants were even rarer. Nathan couldn't recall the last time a new family had moved here. Might have been the Wilcutts when they bought the old mill store and converted it to a pool hall/saloon.

The door opened just a crack, and Nathan noticed the chain had been latched. A pretty face peered out at him. From his limited point of view, she appeared to be in her thirties and have captivating dark eyes. At least one of them.

"Can I help you?" she asked in a big-city voice that sounded very sophisticated. She also seemed a little skittish, like she wasn't used to living outside of suburbia. Could be the solitude was getting to her. But if that was the case after just one day, this poor lady was in for a long haul.

He smiled warmly. "Just thought I'd stop by and welcome you to Blayton."

She surveyed his khaki-colored uniform along with the gun in his holster. "You're the sheriff?"

He extended his plate. "Nathan Thorpe. Nice to meet you."

"Since when do cops bring cookies?" a girl asked over the woman's shoulder.

She turned and whispered back to a shorter person Nathan took to be her daughter. "I don't know."

Now there were two dark eyes in the door crack, one of them belonging to a face that was younger. Boy, city folk were weird. He'd nearly forgotten that part.

"Uh," Nathan began uncertainly, hedging his way back toward the stairs. "I can just leave these on the steps."

"Wait! Don't go." The door slammed shut, and he heard the chain slide off. A split second later, it opened again, and a stunning brunette greeted him. She was petite and wore jeans and a long-sleeved T-shirt. The teenage daughter beside her was dressed in a similar way, but her jeans were torn. Nathan gathered this was the fashion, and not that the girl had fallen and scraped her knees. He'd seen other kids dress like this as well. Thrift-store chic, his niece called it. "I'm so sorry. I… We…didn't mean to be rude. It's just that we weren't expecting anybody."

"Perfectly fine. I understand." He reached in his wallet and flipped open his credentials. "If it makes you feel any better, this proves I'm the real McCoy." He handed them over, still holding the cookie plate in his left hand.

"I can take that," the girl offered helpfully. Though he surmised it was because she'd caught a whiff of chocolate chips. Nathan's cookies had taken first prize at the county fair for three years running. Not that he ever bragged on himself. Other people did it for him.

Nathan passed her the cookies as the mom flipped shut his credentials and returned them. "I apologize for giving you a hard time." She had a youthful face, but those tell-tale crinkles around her eyes said she'd spent a lot of time worrying. Nathan knew it must be hard raising a girl on her own. The high school secretary said there hadn't even been a father's name listed on the matriculation form. He set his jaw in sympathy for this family, knowing that deadbeat dads weren't just a big-city ailment. Sadly, they were commonplace everywhere.

"I don't blame you for being cautious," he said kindly. "In fact, caution's often a good thing."

"Especially at three-way stops," the girl cut in.

"Exactly." His eyes twinkled and Elizabeth couldn't help but notice their shade, a heady mixture of blue and brown with just a hint of green around the irises. An unusual blend of color complemented by his uniform and tawny brown hair. He appeared to be about her age and was incredibly handsome, solid across the chest with a lean, athletic build. He tipped his hat toward Claire. "Nice to see we've got another good driver in town. I've got my hands full with the bad ones."

"Oh no, I don't—"

"She doesn't drive yet," Elizabeth rushed in, her words overlapping with Claire's. She smiled sweetly at her daughter. "But the time's coming soon."

"I'm sure she'll do fine." He shot each a cordial smile.

"I'm sorry," the woman said politely. "I'm Elizabeth Jennings. And this is my daughter, Claire."

"Pleasure," he said with a nod. "I didn't mean to keep you. Just wanted to let you know that I'm here, if you ever need anything."

Elizabeth's gaze inadvertently traveled to his left hand. At least, she thought her gaze was inadvertent. Surely she wasn't checking for a ring. Although she couldn't help but notice, there wasn't one. Not even a tan line left from where one might have been.

"How will we reach you?" Elizabeth asked.

He shot her a grin and her old-enough-to-know-better heart fluttered.

"Dial 9-1-1."

"Isn't that for emergencies?"

His brow rose in a pleased expression. "Will you be calling me otherwise?"

Elizabeth's cheeks flamed. "I meant, just in case it's something minor. A question, maybe."

He cocked his chin to the side. "9-1-1 will do. We don't get many true emergencies. Martha won't mind."

"Martha?"

"She mans the phones and for the most part spends her days extremely bored. I'm sure she'd welcome the chance to chat with you."

Elizabeth eyed him uncertainly. "Well, all right, if you're sure."

"Wouldn't be opposed myself," he muttered, turning away.

Elizabeth leaned out the door. "What's that?"

His neck colored slightly as he set his eyes on hers. "I said, call any time. No question is too big or too small."

"Ask him, Mom," her daughter urged.

"Do you know anything about the house next door?"

"The old Fenton place?" he asked, intrigued. "I know everything about it. Why?"

"We thought we saw someone in there," Claire said.

"Or something," Elizabeth added quickly. "Of course, it could have been just some shadows."

"What about the light?" Claire prodded with obvious concern.

"Light?"

"There was a sliver of something," Elizabeth said. "I don't know. It was too early for moonlight. I saw it too."

"Hmm." Nathan reached up and stroked his chin. "Could it have looked like this…?" He unhitched the flashlight from his belt and clicked it on, spreading broad beams across the stoop's floorboards.

Elizabeth swallowed hard. "You mean someone was in there? A person?"

Nathan appeared mildly amused. "Most certainly." He clicked off the flashlight, then clipped it back to his belt. "That was me."

"You?" Elizabeth and Claire asked in unison.

"Bob Robeson, the realtor, gave me a key. I stop by to check in once in a while. Ensure nothing is amiss."

Elizabeth felt her stomach churn. "Amiss how?"

"Nothing to trouble over," he answered. "Kid stuff. This time of year, especially. Sometimes teens play pranks. Dare each other to sneak inside and then spend the night. Nobody's ever made it, as far as I can tell."

"Is the place haunted?" Claire asked in all seriousness.

Nathan perused her kindly. "The house is old, sure. With a couple of strange legends attached. But haunted? Not likely."

Elizabeth was about to ask about those strange legends but stopped herself. Claire seemed on edge enough as it was. No need to go upsetting her child further with some idle, small-town lore. Besides, if Nathan assured them nothing was wrong, then what did the two of them have to worry about? He seemed an upright enough individual and was a man of the law besides.

"We appreciate you stopping by," she told him.

"And thanks for the cookies," Claire added.

"No problem, ladies. Enjoy the rest of your evening."

Then he walked down the path and cut across the neighbor's yard, heading to the drive around back.

"Where's his cruiser?" Claire asked.

"He probably parked it behind the house." She shut the door and locked it up tight, turning the dead bolt and sliding the chain in place for extra security.

"That was nice of him to bring cookies," Claire said.

"Yes," Elizabeth agreed. "Why don't we have a few with two cold glasses of milk?"

Later that night, Elizabeth walked to the window to draw the blinds as she prepared for bed. Across the country road abutting her house sat the empty graveyard. Moonlight glinted off tombstones as a hoot owl called. The window was up just a tad to let in the breeze and freshen the air. Though this house couldn't be more than five years old, it smelled as musty and stale as an old cupboard. A floorboard creaked, and

Elizabeth's heart pounded. Her gaze traveled to the side window facing the neighboring house. The rockers next door swayed gently in soft gusts of wind. Now who's letting her imagination get the best of her?

Elizabeth tugged shut the window, thinking she'd never sleep a wink hearing things go creak in the night. Suddenly, something caught her eye, and her blood ran cold. There, straight in her line of vision and at the highest point on the hill, sat two newly dug graves. It seemed impossible that she could have missed them before, mounds of fresh earth heaped high upon each, but she couldn't recall having seen them at all. Elizabeth scolded herself for being spooked by what was obviously a routine occurrence. Of course people were buried there. She just hadn't expected to take a daily head count.

Thank goodness their stay here was only temporary and that she wouldn't need to worry over their imperfect dwelling for too long. As soon as she was able, she'd investigate alternate lodging. In the meantime, she had other priorities. Claire started school on Monday, and Elizabeth had serious work to do. She had the key to the old newspaper shop and planned to make the place gleam like new.

~ End of Excerpt *~*

The Light at the End of the Road
A woman is stranded along a lonely Virginia road
and a handsome stranger comes to her aid.

Chapter One

Samantha Williams centered her hands on the
steering wheel and peered through the windshield. Fog
crept up the glass as ice streaked it from the outside.
The windshield wipers whipped back and forth, battling
the frigid onslaught. Sam reached out a hand to adjust
the windshield defroster, cranking it up a notch until it
gusted full blast. Inch by inch, the dark road became
visible beneath an arc of clearing fog, headlights
haunting the eerie path before her. She hadn't seen
another car in more than forty miles.

This wasn't the route Sam normally took at night.
She certainly wouldn't have selected it on purpose,
given the dangerous weather. Sam rarely took back
roads home anymore. But a tractor-trailer had
jackknifed along a steep incline on Highway 64,
tumbling sideways and dislodging barrels of hazardous
chemicals. One of the officers from the highway
barricade had told her about it, recommending she take
a detour. He suggested even more strongly that she get
off the road. This early spring ice storm had caught
everyone by surprise, including the Virginia Highway
Patrol, he'd said with a polite smile and a tip of his hat.

But Sam didn't have the luxury of waiting for the
expected midday thaw that would occur fourteen hours

later, or even until daybreak. Her father's life hung in the balance, and she needed to be by his side. Besides, it wasn't like there was ready lodging in these parts. She'd passed the last motel an hour ago and the small, roadside gas stations, some of them housing country stores, all closed by nine p.m. Some even may have shuttered down earlier with word of the impending storm. Sam was glad she'd stopped to fill her gas tank when she had.

Sam viewed the rugged mountains in the distance. Soon she'd have to cross them, and the curves that were already starting to bend at the foothills' base would become even more daunting, the drop-offs beneath them precipitous. Sam tried not to think about that, and focused instead on the road ahead, tightening her fingers around the wheel. *One step at a time* was all she needed to conquer. In another two hours, she'd see the light her mother kept burning in the window at home.

Lisa replaced the small bulb in the short plastic candle in the front hall window. It was the sort that people put out at Christmastime. The year Sam's brother Jimmy went missing at sea was the year she'd left one candle out when she'd packed the rest of the Christmas decorations away. Affable and good-looking, Jimmy had possessed a natural way of charming the ladies—beginning with his kindergarten teacher, who had assured his parents Jimmy was destined to do great things. He'd grown up in a popular crowd, his friends coming and going throughout their busy household day after day. Jimmy played football and was a star swimmer. When he'd announced his desire to become a Navy Seal, then won his scholarship to the U.S. Naval Academy, none of his teachers was surprised.

Jimmy had ambition and a plan, unlike his sister, who had talent yet no goals. Quiet and introspective like her father, Sam took longer to come into her own. She'd been a happy child with a few close friends, but didn't decide to pursue art professionally until college. There she'd met a photography professor she admired, and the rest was history. She'd made a wonderful career for herself, and Ben and Lisa couldn't have been more proud. If only Jimmy were around to see it.

Something raw caught in Lisa's throat and she drew in a sniff. They were never told exactly what had happened to Jimmy, only that he'd died bravely, serving his country. At times, thoughts of his death overwhelmed her. Mostly, Lisa forced herself not to think about it at all because the pain ran too deep.

She sank weakly into a living room chair, also thinking of Ben. Lisa wasn't sure how she could move forward without the two of them. Though Ben had promised her she would. "Be a good wife and bring me some Scotch," he'd said, dragging his thumb across her cheek. He'd caught a tear there, but pretended not to notice. "You'll be okay, hon. No matter what. You've got Sam." Yes, but Sam was a young woman with a life of her own, and Lisa would never interfere with that.

They'd been discussing Ben's condition, which seemed to be getting worse—even after triple-bypass surgery and his staying on medication. Lisa had been urging Ben to return to the doctor, but he kept putting it off, saying he would go just as soon as he got some important project wrapped up.

"You're not supposed to drink Scotch and you know it."

"Right." He gave her a wry smile, blue eyes dancing beneath a mop of silvery hair. "Could shave another fifteen minutes off at the end."

"Ben!" she said, aghast.

"Who says I'll even want those last fifteen minutes? They could be perfectly dreadful." Ben's illness hadn't deprived him of his sense of humor, or his looks. He still had a commanding presence and a handsome face. The fact that it was etched with wrinkles only made him look more seasoned, like a seafarer of sorts, or someone who'd weathered life's storms. Oh, how Lisa prayed he would weather this one. He pulled her out of her reverie with a quip.

"Better make mine a double."

She laughed lightly and fixed him his drink. Within minutes, she regretted that decision. The glass slipped from his hand, colliding with the carpet as he doubled forward, gripping his arm. In a flash, Lisa was on the phone dialing 9-1-1. The EMTs arrived quickly, then Ben was whisked away to the hospital in an ambulance.

After a quick consultation with his surgeon, he was being admitted to the hospital and prepped for emergency surgery. Another open-heart operation was risky, coming so close on the heels of his previous one. But at the moment, it was the only option they had. Lisa rushed home to gather Ben's things and place a few calls. She wondered if she'd been right in alerting Sam on such a treacherous night, though she sensed that her daughter never would have forgiven her if she hadn't.

Lisa stared out the window at the icy rain, knowing Sam was doing everything in her power to get home. Lisa had tried to dissuade her from traveling tonight, begging her to wait until tomorrow, when the roads would be clearer. But Sam wouldn't hear of it. She was her daddy's girl.

"Put your coat on and come with me, Sam."

Six-year-old Sam looked up at her dad, twin pigtails skimming each shoulder. She had honey-colored hair like her mom's, but her sky-blue eyes were her dad's. "Where are we going, Papa?" Her mom looked up from her knitting on the sofa, her raised brow asking the same question.

"To see some *magic*." He winked at his wife and Lisa laughed, apparently remembering something they'd shared earlier.

Sam eagerly slipped on her coat, sensing another adventure. Her dad was full of them. She especially loved adventuring with him at night. He worked for a big telescope lab and sometimes took trips to exotic-sounding places. Mostly, though, he worked remotely from the regional office nearby, which allowed him to do what he enjoyed most: spending time with his family. When Jimmy was younger, he liked these adventures too. Now that Jimmy was in high school and into sports and girls, things had changed. So it was often just Sam who accompanied Papa on his missions.

"Don't keep her out too late!" her mom cautioned as they slipped out the door. "School tomorrow!"

"One can't always predict the stars, my love."

"I beg to differ." Lisa smiled softly. "I seem to know a gentleman who can."

Ben gave a low chuckle, then tugged the door shut behind them, leading Sam toward the truck. "We're going to Barrett's Field?" she asked, excited by the possibilities. Only the most spectacular things happened there. Like when Sam witnessed her first meteor shower. Her dad had roused her at four in the morning for that one. Her mom really was a good sport. Even though she never wanted to come along, she seemed content to let Sam have fun.

An hour later, Sam shivered beneath the truck blanket as she sat on the edge of a haystack.

Her dad quit fiddling with his field telescope. "Too cold for you?" he asked with concern.

"Uh-uh," Sam lied, little puffs of breath hovering above her lips. She stared up at a bright object glittering like a diamond. "What's that one, Papa?"

"Polaris. The North Star." He smiled warmly. "If you ever get lost, it can help lead you home."

"How?"

"It's true north. Always has been, always will be."

Ben checked his watch, then adjusted the telescope, sharpening the focus of the lens. "Aha!"

Sam sucked in a breath, unable to bear the suspense. He hadn't told her what they'd come for, but it was bound to be big. Her father motioned her closer and she took her position before the scope. A grainy globe danced across her field of vision, in very slow motion as if it were swimming underwater. Only it was dragging something long behind it, shimmering and wonderful, like the train on her Aunt Beth's wedding dress. Sam had served as a flower girl just last year.

She pulled back from the eyepiece to catch her father wearing a broad grin. "You can even see it with the naked eye. Beautiful, isn't she?"

Sam stared into the rich, sparkly night sky studded with stars, and one gloriously dancing bride. "She looks just like Aunt Beth."

Ben chuckled aloud, getting it immediately. "A bride? Hmm." He thoughtfully stroked his chin. "I like that name for a comet, but this one already belongs to someone."

"What do you mean?"

"The astronomer who found her first got to name her."

"Wow."

She shot him a hopeful look. "Will you name something after me?"

He smiled and thumbed her nose. "Someday? Most certainly."

Moisture gathered in Sam's eyes as she recalled her dad's high-school graduation gift. Not only was he funding her attendance at a prestigious state university; he'd also presented her with something far more personal. He'd studied twin planets somewhere in a faraway galaxy. One had a previously undiscovered moon. Due to its fixed orbit, it stayed brightly illuminated at all times. He'd named it Sam's Bride. Her dad had joked that some day in the future, folks might speculate about a space explorer named Sam and admire his marital tribute, never knowing the true origin of the name.

Sam's back wheels slipped suddenly and she clutched the steering wheel as the anti-skid control mechanism kicked in. Heaving a breath, Sam decided she needed to pay more attention to her driving and less to her memories, but they were hard to put aside. An ache rose in her chest so fierce that it burned. Sam couldn't lose her dad now, she just couldn't. More tears pooled, blurring her vision for a fraction of a second too long. *No!* She quickly righted her path, steering her car back into the center of her lane. There was barely any shoulder here, and the terrain was getting steeper. Just a few more miles, and she'd be over this ridge.

~ End of Excerpt *~*

Ginny Baird thanks you for reading her work and hopes to hear from you soon!

47377528R00155

Made in the USA
Charleston, SC
10 October 2015